TREBLE DEATH

MUSICAL MAYHEM BOOK 3

KM JACKWAYS

OLD SOULS PRESS

Published by Old Souls Press

A catalogue record for this book is available from the National Library of New Zealand

ISBN

[978-1-0670250-0-7] (kindle)

[978-1-0670250-2-1] (ebook)

[978-1-0670250-1-4] (paperback)

Sign up for the author's newsletter on the website to be the first to hear of new releases: www.kimjackways.com

❀ Created with Vellum

For the dreamers, the treasure-gatherers, and those who believe in the magic of everyday things

CHAPTER 1

*A*n almost tangible excitement crackled around the tavern. Ledstow hadn't seen an event like the Talent Quest in many years. There was scarcely any room to move in the Twig and Berries pub and Jeremiah, the barman, was almost dancing, as he moved from the post-mix hose to the fridge to the tap to pull a pint of beer.

Esther planted her feet hip width apart, pushed out her chest and breathed deep into her core. The first notes came to her and she belted them out. No one looked twice at her in the noisy hubbub as she sang the chorus of 'Crow', the new song she had written, holding onto the note for one, two, three beats.

A wine glass swung slowly on the rack above the

bar, making a tick tick noise. *Must be a breeze in here*, she thought.

She repeated her line, concentrating on feeling the tone since she couldn't hear herself properly. As she held onto the F, there came a rattling sound, and she looked up. Glasses were rocking upwards along the metal fingers towards the end. She pointed up and made an incoherent noise, accidentally poking Ashton in the nose as he leaned in to say something. She gestured to him and he turned to look, just as two glasses swung over the end of the hooks and hung for a second, like some cartoon character who hadn't yet looked down as they skedaddled through the air, before plummeting towards the ground.

Esther watched in horror while Jeremiah, his long hair tied back in a man bun, made a cocktail directly beneath the ill-fated glassware. But he simply snatched up the two glasses from the air, one in each hand, a moment before they smashed onto the bar, placing them neatly on the wooden surface. He gave her a wink, before turning away to serve a customer.

She let out a shaky breath. "Crotchets!"

"Nice save! Was that from your… woo woo?" Ashton wiggled his fingers at her.

"I think so. I don't even know any more."

"Well, maybe don't do whatever you did?" he said. "It might make it hard for the audience to appreciate our bangin' music if a shower of glass rains down upon them."

"Really helpful there, Ash. I can't exactly control it. My grandmother said that when you first come into your magic, it can sort of surge in waves," she whispered fiercely. "It happens when I sing sometimes."

"Sounds like my sister. She's going through menopause and has to stand by the open fridge while cooking tea. Because of the hot flushes. They come in waves." He saw her face and patted her arm. "I'm joking, alright? Just relax. It was fine the whole time we were practising. That was just a one-off, I'm sure of it."

She let out a breath. "I hope so. What's the time again? I've got time to go to the bathroom, don't I?"

"Yeah," he said, looking at his phone. "Maybe go and stand in the fridge for a minute and see if it helps you, too."

Esther threw him a look, then threaded her way through the people chatting and laughing. A small stage was set up in the corner of the dining area and the tables had been pushed back towards the walls so there was room around the stage. The folding doors had been opened up to include the snug. At least she was familiar with the pub from their many nights here singing karaoke. That would make the performance a little easier.

On her way to the bathrooms, she heard raised

voices coming from the kitchen. It sounded like arguing and she peeked through the doors to see what was happening. Well, she resisted for a few seconds first, pausing in the middle of the corridor, pretending to look at the pictures on the wall, before pressing her nose up to the glass. She wasn't a complete busybody.

Inside were two chefs in white, heads down, steadfastly looking at their pans of food. Nothing suspect so far. A large walk-in chiller. She moved to the side and could see Jeremiah shooting daggers at the young lady that waited tables and worked in the bar. They were standing about a metre apart and seemed to be arguing about a plate of food. Perhaps the chefs were concentrating a little too much on what they were doing, as if trying to listen in without letting the others know. She could hardly judge as she was doing the same.

Esther dodged out of the way as the door slammed open. She hurried into the bathrooms.

A few minutes later, when she came back into the noisy tavern, Esther eyed Jeremiah. He now looked perfectly calm as he joked with the customers and prepared drinks with the speed and the precision of an Olympic table tennis player. It might have been her imagination, but the young woman seemed to be keeping her distance. Perhaps her smile seemed a little forced. That was interesting to Esther as the two staff members usually seemed to get on well, from what she could recall.

After a few minutes, Jeremiah lifted up the flap in the bar and bounded up to the front, grabbing the microphone. "Alright. Welcome, everyone, to the Ledstow talent quest. Georgia is looking after the bar so be kind to her," Jeremiah said, pointing at the young woman that Esther had seen in the kitchen. A few people cheered.

"She'll keep you all fed and watered. It might just take a little time as we are a bit busier than usual. I think we're ready to get underway. We have six acts with three songs each. If you haven't registered, you've got about five minutes to do so. The winning act will receive two hundred pounds, a bar tab and something else that's pretty special." An interested murmur rose up from the crowd. "One of our sponsors has offered one full day at a recording studio for our winners. That's three hundred pounds worth. Now, this was very late in the game. If I'd known, I could have advertised it a bit more. But I'm sure you'll all agree it's a great opportunity for our musicians."

Ashton let out a low whistle. "We've got this, Essie," he said, as if it were as simple as winning team Pictionary on one of their game nights.

It was a great prize. Time in a recording studio would mean they could produce a quality-sounding album of their original songs. But Esther was more worried about whether she'd bring the house down. Literally.

♫

HER MAGIC HAD 'COME IN' a few months before, in the run-up to Christmas. She'd discovered, from her grandmother, the inestimable Hope Forte, that musical magic was in her blood, but her memories of anything witchy had been hidden from her when she was a child because of a magical vow. Once the vow was removed, Hope had begun to teach her magic, drawing on what she knew and what she guessed. Esther practised as much as she could but, now and then, a surge of magic caused unpredictable results. It often happened when she was feeling most out of control.

One of these times was when she had joined the local theatre group production just a few months ago, along with her boyfriend Clark, to find out who killed the actor who was the star of the show. While singing the final number in the musical, she'd caused a fellow actress to start shifting into her fox form while right there on the stage. Just because she, Esther, was desperate to learn the truth. While that occasion had turned out fine in the end and had ultimately helped to unmask the killer, it was fair to say that her singing could be hazardous.

So she had reluctantly agreed to do the talent show; for Ashton and because, frankly, she needed money.

Everything was getting more expensive. The rent had gone up. Her boss at the music shop had quietly employed his nephew, which meant that Esther had fewer shifts. Knowing her boss, if he was giving shifts to his relative, he must be paying the kid even less than Esther. That could hardly even be legal.

Then there was the incident that she had called the Great Flood. She had come home from music practise to find water all over the floor in the kitchen and creeping into the lounge. While fetching old towels and buckets to stem the flow, she noticed that the washing machine pipe, which usually hung into the sink, was swinging free and pumping water out into the flat. Neither of the pets had owned up, but Esther strongly suspected Louis. The landlord had taken one long look, said he would be in touch with his insurance company, and told her to brace for a bill.

When Ashton came over to her flat talking about a talent quest with a cash prize that was 'theirs for the taking', she couldn't refuse. They had entered the competition just a few days ago, with two covers and one original piece, Crow. Esther had written the lyrics and music for their original song while sitting in her flat one night, with a glass of wine in one hand.

The words came first and then the melody came easily, fitting into the mood of each line. Everything came together. As she had played, Jay flitted over and perched on the next chair, tweaking at her shoulder when she stopped to work out a note. Then she had video-called Ashton and played him the chorus. From the sound that he made, that he later strongly denied was screaming, she figured it must be good.

"It's not too personal?" She'd asked. "It feels too personal."

"Nah. I bet even The Beatles thought that, sometimes. People will love it."

♫

"Give these guys all your support," Georgia yelled now, as a group of three middle-aged men, clad in denim and with long, shaggy hair took the stage for the first act.

"We are The Revolting Tenors," a man with a fluffy red beard boomed into the microphone. "We're rising up against the man. With music."

"Uh oh," Ashton said, half-covering his face with his hand, as Red Beard stepped forward and opened his mouth to sing a verse in a mellow voice.

"I don't think these guys are too much of a threat," Esther responded. "I mean, it's a good beat. But otherwise…"

Ash shook his head. "No, it's not that."

The volume rose as the group got to the chorus and brought in a heavy metal beat that thudded through the floor.

"What?"

He leaned closer and she could see the scar on his cheekbone from a childhood incident with a fishing knife. "It's bloody Ham Falkirk," he said.

The name jogged something in her memory from Ash's stories. "The guy at the front? Wait a minute. Is that the kid who flushed your Tamagotchi? Back in Bristol?"

He looked up. "I don't have any proof," he answered, a dark expression crossing his face. "But yeah, it was him. I loved that little clump of pixels."

"How old were you?"

"Eight."

"He's here in Ledstow?"

"Apparently. He could be living in any of the towns nearby, I suppose."

"What? Oh yeah, true."

"Anything I did, he did too. I sung in the school talent show. The next year he sung a song by the same artist. At high school, I joined the debate club and he somehow managed to be captain of the rival team. Their team won and went to the finals and he let me know all about it. He was a royal pain."

"This is a good chance to ask him for your Tamagotchi back," Esther yelled, just as the music dropped away. A few people turned and gave her curious stares. She flashed them a nervous smile.

The music turned out to be a mix of country and metal, heavy in places, but mostly very easy to listen to. It wasn't wonderful, but Esther was all about supporting fellow artists, so she clapped and cheered when they finished their set.

Ash looked at her, while clapping. "We're next."

CHAPTER 2

With those ominous words, Esther grabbed her ukulele and her music sheets and slapped her hat on her head.

Their friends were already on the stage, setting up the equipment for them. Troy was leaning down, adjusting the microphone stand. Aria patted her on the back in quiet solidarity.

"Start whenever you like, guys," Jeremiah said.

Ashton picked up his guitar with a flourish and introduced them, as they had practised. "Hi everyone. I'm Ash and I'm one half of Soulful. We're available to sing covers for your next live event." With an exaggerated bow, he stepped out of the way.

Esther hurried onto the little stage and took the

microphone. "And I'm Esther. Um, we have an original song too now, I guess, which we'll play last. Enjoy."

She turned to Ashton and played a few notes. He smiled at her and sung the first line of their version of *Fast Car* by Tracy Chapman in his smooth voice. Esther harmonised with him and relaxed into the melody as she could see the audience enjoying it. It was an emotional song that evoked difficult childhoods and the sweet promise of escape into a better life, a song about learning and strength and hope and first love. It reminded her of how far she'd come. She forgot who and where she was as the music channeled through her, only coming back to the present when the applause started.

Next they played their cover of Bob Dylan's *All Along the Watchtower* that had quickly become a favourite among their friends. It suited Ashton's strong tenor voice.

To her, this song was about balancing the magical world and this one. What did that really mean, though? It wasn't like she could model off her mother or her grandmother. One had been bound by a vow never to talk about witchcraft and the other chose to keep it a secret to fit in with her social circle. Esther would have to find her own way to live her life in the watchtower, while paranormal happenings, hauntings, and murders beset her town.

Ash elbowed her and she realised the song was over. She took a sip of water from her bottle while Ash spoke.

"This next one is really special. It's an original song written by Esther here."

She nodded. "It's called Crow and it's about the strength that quiet people have and how that's sometimes not recognised." She paused, and took a long breath. Some people shuffled.

"Is it happening again?" Ash hissed.

She shook her head. The problem wasn't her magic this time. It was that she was so invested in this piece of her soul. Would the crowd get it? She rubbed her fingers over damp palms.

"Not all who fly are peaceful,
Not all who nest are gentle
Some of us are wise, you know
I'm just a crow"

She faltered. A sea of blank faces stared back at her. She *was* an imposter.

"Boo," someone yelled.

"We want covers!"

Esther kept singing, but she felt that if her magic had come in right then, the small stage would have collapsed into a sinkhole and swallowed her and Ash right up. She felt as if her face and body had turned to plastic.

"That was always going to happen at some point," Ash reassured her as they bowed. "People like the songs they know. That's why artists do covers. Once they hear it a few times, they'll love it. Don't worry about it."

"Yeah, I know you're right." She answered in a flat voice. She somehow made it off the stage and fell heavily into her chair.

"I'll order you a drink."

"Thanks."

Aria squeezed her hand.

The gin in her drink slowly warmed her up again as she watched. The next two acts were a soft rock band singing covers and a group of a cappella singers. People clapped politely after each.

"I think we've got a chance here," Ash said to her.

She shrugged.

From the front, Jeremiah let out a whistle to catch everyone's attention. "I hope everyone is comfortable and has a drink in their hands. We've got something special next. This one was a surprise to me most of all. In a good way."

Georgia climbed around from behind the bar and ran up the front. She bent to pick up something from a bag next to the stage. She stepped onto the wooden planks, holding the object behind her back and nervously tucked her blonde hair behind her ear. Nobody was paying her much attention. A curl bounced back onto her face and she dragged it back.

"Apron," Jeremiah called, waving a hand.

Georgia looked down. She quickly took off the item and bundled it up into a ball, then turned back to the audience. She whipped an instrument out and held it up. Esther recognised the pan flute. A few people laughed.

Closing her eyes, she brought the pipes to her mouth. She took a deep breath in and a pregnant hush fell over the crowd as they waited for her to play.

"Did you know?" Georgia demanded, instead, raising her voice over the crowd's cries of 'get on with it'. "The pan flute was named for the Greek god Pan. He fell in love with a nymph" — here, she curtsied low — "with a beautiful singing voice. He pursued her relentlessly. Guys, no means no, alright? Until… finally she cast herself into the river."

She closed her eyes again and threw back her head then played the first eight notes of a melody. Esther could tell it was *The Sound of Silence*. It was a good description of the room, which was filled with people of all ages, struck dumb by the spectacle. The woman next to her had her mouth open.

Georgia gave them a grin, breaking character for a moment, which led to a round of applause. She was good! Esther wished she had that sort of crowd control.

"The poor nymph went to her sisters, who turned her into a reed to get away from his advances. But the wind blew and the beautiful sound in the reeds reminded him of the nymph's singing. He cut down the reeds in a fit of rage. And voilà! We have the pan flute."

Without missing a beat, she continued the song. It took them across haunting moors, to the top of a lonely mountain and back again, through a long marriage and a widow's keening. The woman next to her had eyes shiny with tears.

Ash turned to her. "Oh, shit."

This was precisely what Esther was thinking as she watched the performance and the way Georgia held almost everyone in the room in the palm of her hand.

Not quite everyone, she realised. Jeremiah had his back turned to the performance, checking and restocking the refrigerator.

The song finished and the room erupted into cheers that continued for a long while.

"Well, who knew that my staff had such serious talent?" Jeremiah boomed. "While you all wet your whistle, we'll do the hard work and mark each act."

"There's always next time," Aria said to her, as if it was already a fact that they hadn't won.

It was only a few minutes later when Jeremiah called out again.

"Our judges have deliberated. Please bear in mind that they are looking for something with wide appeal. The winners will be announced by the execs from the recording studio, Vi and Cheryl."

There was a polite smatter of applause and two well-dressed people stepped up to the front. One had pale skin with a severe red bob hairstyle that accentuated her cheekbones and one was slender and tall, with black skin and long silky hair.

The one with red hair spoke. "Hello everyone, I'm Cheryl. We thought all of the acts were wonderful. What a wealth of talent you have in Ledstow. In third place, we have The Revolting Tenors, that's Hamish, Andrew and George. This was a very interesting take on the genre. In second place..." She looked down to check her notes. "Soulful."

The room erupted in clapping, catcalls and hooting.

"Quiet, everyone. Esther and Ashton gave us an emotional performance. We really enjoyed it."

Second. That was nothing to sniff at. Esther smiled at her friends.

The black woman stepped forwards and stood with her hands behind her back. "And in first place, we have the amazing Georgia Haddock. We were absolutely shocked to hear it was her first ever public performance and wish her the best of luck for the future."

There was a stunned silence.

Then Georgia vaulted over the bar and ran up to the stage. "Oh, thank you so much!"

"Oh well, we gave it our best shot, Ash," Esther said, after the applause had died down.

"We came second. Let's just have another round—"

She looked up to see what had caught his attention.

Ham Falkirk was passing by, carrying an amp, and he stared at them as he passed.

"What *is* his problem?" she asked. "So he didn't win. Neither did we."

"You were both flipping awesome tonight and you know it," Aria said. "It just wasn't to be."

"It was stolen," Ash said. "Youth won over beauty."

Esther laughed. "If I knew about sports, I'd say something like 'she came out of left field'."

"No, really. Good for her."

They finished their drinks, listening to Aria's work story about a hotel customer who came down to breakfast in the restaurant half-dressed.

"Alright, I'm going to call it," Esther said. "I'm going home to bed." She gathered up her things.

"I'll probably leave now too," Ash said.

The evening was cool but calm, with a slight breeze that tickled the hair around her ears.

"I thought it was you, Ashton." The man with the red beard smiled broadly. "How have you been?"

"Not bad, not bad. And you, Ham?" She could see that Ash was uncomfortable and racked her brains for an excuse to leave.

"Oh, you know. This is my BMW."

"Come up in the world a bit, haven't you?"

Esther saw a friendly face that instantly made her feel better and left Ash chatting awkwardly.

"Did I miss it?" Clark said, crossing the road. "I did, I'm sorry. I'll make it up to you." He squeezed her hand. "We'll go have a nice lunch this week."

"That's ok. You had to work," she said. "It went mostly well. It was just the song that I wrote that they didn't like."

"Correction," Ash said from beside her. "They don't like it yet! They will. We could really have done with that recording time, though."

"Yeah," she agreed. And the money. It was time to go back to the drawing board.

CHAPTER 3

Esther, swallowing back bitter hubris, had to admit that her mother was right. She switched on the water to boil, staring out at the grey morning, phone pressed to her ear.

"I think you need to look for a better job," her mother's voice broke through her thoughts. "It's time. You've done your stint in retail. That job was only a stepping stone, anyway. We've got tennis friends who might be able to find you something better."

"There aren't a lot of jobs here in Ledstow," she replied. "I don't think your tennis friends can conjure jobs up out of thin air."

There was a pause, and Esther imagined that her mum was pursing her lips, as she usually did at Esther's flippant mentions of magical happenings. "Well, you might need to travel a bit for work or you might even have to move. We used to make do, you know, when we were first married. Did what we had to. There were no fancy coffees or squashed avocado on toast. We only ate out once a year."

"Smashed. It's smashed avocado," Esther said, thinking of how her mother had bought her first house at twenty-one years old. "Let me guess, buying a house cost eight hundred pounds back then? Anyway, I'm busy right now. I have to go."

"Six thousand, actually. It was a lot of money back then. Wait a minute. I was going to say that you could always get another flatmate. You've got that spare room there, where Aria used to sleep."

The toaster popped and Esther reached for the two thick slices of toast. She spread some crumbly feta on top and added sliced cherry tomatoes. The cheese smell made her mouth water. She topped it with salt and cracked black pepper. It wasn't quite smashed avocado, but it would do.

"Have I? No, I don't think there's a spare room," she said. "Louis wouldn't like me renting out his room. Poor little kitty. And I'm not moving away and leaving nan in Ledstow all alone."

"Esther! Why don't you come over here and visit us

and we'll see what we can do. And bring that policeman of yours."

"Can't you just email me the details?"

"I do enough emailing at work. Part of your problem is that you need to front up to things in person. So… This Saturday will work. It'll be nice."

The 'nice' had just enough emphasis that she couldn't really refuse. It was one small word that contained multitudes. Perhaps it would lead to a good opportunity.

"Alright, fine. See you then." She poured two cups of strong tea and put the plate of toast on a wooden tray.

"Looking forward to meeting him properly," her mother trilled.

Esther sighed, putting the phone down. She picked up the tray and went through to the bedroom.

"This is luxurious." Clark was sitting up in the bed, shirtless, the sheet bunched around his waist.

"You're easy to please."

He nodded, munching on a mouthful of toast.

She leaned against his other side. "You have been summoned," she said, rather dramatically. "You can learn first hand about my villain origin story."

"Of course I'll go and meet your parents," he murmured.

A buzzing came from underneath the pillow and Esther reached underneath and passed Clark his phone.

Looking at the screen, he muttered, "work". He quickly swallowed his last mouthful, answered it, and talked with a grim expression on his face.

Esther thought back to the conversation with her mother. Her finances really weren't sustainable. Maybe she would have to think about renting out that room. But the thought of sharing with someone she didn't know? With the kitten and the bird and the witchcraft? She shuddered.

Clark ended the call and turned to her, rubbing the stubble on his chin. "There goes my free time for the foreseeable future. We've got another dead body."

She stared back at him. It had only been two months since the last one. *Let this one be from natural causes, at least.*

Once Clark left, Esther took her time showering and getting dressed. She pulled on a soft jumper and skirt.

"I know, Louis. I should have fed you first." She said this to her cat, a fluffy silver kitten, who was sitting next to his bowl, fixing her with a grumpy stare. She searched through the pantry for a sachet of his gourmet meat. "How dare the humans eat first? Alright, I'm coming up empty here. But don't worry."

She then stretched up into the top storage cupboard,

where she kept the emergency stocks, but her hand reached only bare wood.

Walking past him, she put on her coat, avoiding the cat's gaze. She did need a few other groceries, too. The cat didn't own her.

"Oh, who am I kidding?" She asked, out loud, as she stepped out of her front door.

"Everyone," her neighbour called. "Never take anything seriously, these young people."

"Good morning, Mr Bauer," she replied, sweetly. He was a lovely neighbour really, despite the gruff exterior.

"Hmph."

It was a damp morning when nature wasn't sure if it was still winter or yet spring. Some trees were beginning to blossom, while a chill wind shook last night's rain off the branches of the oak trees above her.

A noisy commotion in the main street beckoned her so she turned down there. A little detour couldn't hurt.

Two police cars were parked haphazardly in the narrow street. A group of people were standing outside The Twig and Berries, some of them in their nightclothes.

"Morning. What's going on?" she asked an old woman.

The woman pointed to the police cars. "They're talking to the young fellow in there. I heard that there's been a death and that it might have been a murder." The last word was offered in a stage whisper.

Esther's heart sank. It had been almost eight weeks since the last one. Was she cursed? And it was in the very place where she'd been last night, too.

"Oh no. Why do you think that?" she asked.

"I live next door to Lea here, who lives next door to the pub." The woman signalled to the row of tiny flats. The short woman next to her nodded enthusiastically. "And she heard them knocking at the door first thing. It took a while for him to come down, didn't it?"

Come down? Esther was confused for a moment, then she realised that they must be talking about Jeremiah living in a flat above the bar. That would make sense. He seemed to be working in the pub at any and all times of the day. She had often seen him in the window, cleaning up or checking the cupboards first thing in the morning. But who was deceased? His wife?

"I'm Lea," the short woman said, putting out her hand. "It was one heck of a noise this morning."

"Must have been for you to hear it," her friend said. "How many years have I been telling you to get a hearing aid?"

"Oh, probably as long as I've been telling you to get one of these." She patted the red mobility scooter that she was standing next to.

"Jeremiah's a lovely lad. He brings us the leftover food from the pub sometimes."

"Wonderful blackberry crumble."

The other woman nodded. "And the bread and butter pudding is to die for!"

Lea screwed up her face. "That's for the birds."

"It is not. You've always been fussy."

"More like discerning."

While they were arguing, Jeremiah appeared at the door, dressed in a grey hooded sweatshirt and tartan pyjama pants, and two police officers came through after him and headed for their car. One of them was Clark and he spotted her.

She stepped to the side to get some distance from the two women, who were looking on, with their eyebrows raised, doubtless impressed at her unexpected source of information.

Clark rubbed at his eyes. It looked like the morning had taken a toll on him.

"Who was it?" she asked. "Who died?"

"It was a lady called Georgia who worked here. Suspicious circumstances. We've just let her boss know." He rubbed at his forehead.

"Oh no," Esther said, as her heart squeezed, thinking of the vibrant young woman in the talent quest. "It was Georgia who won the contest last night."

"Did she? Well, we have to go," Clark added, with a

quick press of her hand, "but I'll catch up with you after work. It'll be another long day."

He gave her a peck on the cheek and headed for the car. Esther turned back towards the pub to find the two women, eyes trained on her, their arms crossed.

"We heard that," the short woman said to her.

"That copper said it was suspicious."

"That's what they say when they think it might be… you know what."

"What happened?"

Esther tried to leave, but the woman beckoned her closer.

"We've seen him in there, canoodling with that young girl. She must have spurned him, I reckon."

"You saw them…?" She was not going to say the word 'canoodling'. "Kissing?"

"Well no, not outright. But that blonde lady was always there after closing. And I'd often see them in the booth, heads together."

"Really?" There was an age gap between Jeremiah and Georgia. Esther thought it must be around fifteen years. That definitely wasn't unheard of. Love was love, after all. But why sneak around?

"I wouldn't think he'd be capable of it," Lea said.

"He did once refuse to pay a parking ticket!"

"That's hardly the same…"

The women seemed to have lost interest in her

when she didn't give them any further gossip, so Esther crossed the road and headed for the grocery store on the corner. She noticed her hands were shaking as she reached for a basket.

Although she hardly knew Georgia and she was no stranger to murders by now, this one had happened after the talent quest that her band had performed at. This one involved the winner of the contest that she had come second in. This one felt personal.

♫

"You've had a long day," she said, embracing Clark when he came in the door. She gently smoothed away the creases in his brow and he leaned forward to kiss her.

Clark headed for the squashy armchair in the corner. They spent a few nights together each week and that had quickly become 'his chair'. "Yeah. Lots of paperwork and meetings with next of kin. It's draining, that stuff."

"Do you want Coke, beer or something stronger?"

"I think I'll have a beer, thanks."

"What about food?"

"Always. But I can cook, if you like."

Esther appreciated the sentiment but he looked like he might keel over into the kale. "Tomorrow, you can.

I've got something nice and easy ready to go." She went to the kitchen and made a simple meal of homemade burgers, which they ate at the kitchen table, talking of small matters.

It was only much later that she broached the subject that had been nagging at her mind again.

"Have they opened a murder investigation?"

"Not yet. You know how reluctant they are to throw all their resources at it."

"So what happened? I've been thinking about poor Georgia all day."

"Yes, terrible. If there's one good thing about it, it seems like a pretty clear cut case. She was found in the park by someone who lived nearby. We've had someone come forward and say that her partner was quite obsessive. The car was left at the park so we can assume she went there to meet someone she trusted, which fits with the theory as well. Did you say she won the talent quest? What was the prize?"

"Hm?" Esther tilted her head to the side. She was not expecting him to say that Georgia had a boyfriend after the juicy gossip from the women outside the pub. "Oh, a cash prize and time in a recording studio. I don't think it's enough to be a motive. So you suspect her partner?"

"It's only day one, but yes, that's my impression. We will know more once we find a murder weapon or anything else at the site. But right now, I need to think about something else for a while."

"Well, I'll distract you with something much more terrifying. Did you remember that you're coming to meet my parents tomorrow?"

CHAPTER 4

"Are you sure you're ready for this?" Esther asked, as they drove through Paunceworthy and pulled to a stop outside the large house. She could see how the place would be daunting as it looked as if it was straight from the pages of *Country Life* magazine. This would be the first time she'd seen her family since they turned up at the play unannounced.

"Nah, this is going to be fine," he said. "Parents love me."

Oh, you sweet summer child, she thought. "Alright, whatever you say. And please don't mention the investigations. You know what mum does for a job."

"She's a judge," he confirmed, with a grim expression.

Esther rang the bell and the door swung inwards almost immediately.

"Darling," her mother said, leaning forward to kiss her cheek. She shook Clark's hand. "Hello. Nice to meet you."

Her dad appeared at the door and stuck his hand out to shake.

"Hi Paula. Hi Grant. It's good to meet you both," Clark said.

"I hope the drive was alright? It's such an awfully long way for you to get here," her mother said, over her shoulder as she went down the hallway. "I don't know why Esther felt she had to move so far away."

"The drive wasn't too bad at all," Clark answered, squeezing Esther's shoulder in support as they stepped inside.

"Your mother's got me looking after the lunch," her dad said, hurrying back into the kitchen. "Take a seat, you two."

As they were about to sit down, her mum came back into the lounge. She looked at Clark. "Can you give me a wee hand with something? We need some help with moving some things around. And Esther, go and clean out that little chest of drawers of yours. I'm going to sell it as it doesn't fit in with the new colour scheme. I've been waiting to ask you to do that since Christmas."

Esther went up to her old room, nostalgia overcoming her as it did every time, although the walls were now a sage green instead of the mauve she'd loved. She pulled the top drawer out and placed it on the bed. Of course, she'd taken all her valuables and knick knacks out a long time ago but there was still plenty in there; a stack of friendship bracelets, the first CD she ever bought and a folder of souvenirs from her high school band camp.

A photo slipped out onto the bedspread and she picked it up. She and four others were looking at the camera, their eyes squinted shut against the light. They were about fourteen and on band camp. She was a little apart from the others. That was the first time they'd practised conducting and she hadn't done very well. She took the picture and a couple of other things, before sweeping the rest of the stuff into a rubbish bag.

They sat down to eat in the conservatory, the table overladen with platters of food, from beef wellington to roast potatoes to minted green peas.

"So, Clark, are you enjoying spending time with Esther? We certainly don't get a lot of her time."

Esther rolled her eyes so hard it hurt.

"Yes. She's very good at finding clues and solving… ah, puzzles." He frowned and looked across at Esther.

What sort of an answer was that? Sometimes her dearly beloved was very strange. Perhaps he was nervous around new people. But his near mention of murder investigations was about as subtle as a Trojan horse arriving at the city gates.

"Do you like the beef? I bought the tenderloin from the market this morning."

"It's nice," Esther said.

Clark nodded, his mouth full.

"You like Ledstow?" Her father asked.

"It's alright. It can be fascinating. I probably get to see the best and the worst of it in my job."

"As a cop," she put in, quickly. Odd. She thought he loved the little town of Ledstow as much as her.

"Ah yes," her father said. "We have a friend from the golf club who's in the police, as well, don't we? Alexander Riggleton. Do you know him?"

"Dad, he doesn't know every cop in England."

Clark shook his head. "We don't really mix that much with other stations. We're kept pretty busy at home. The only time would be for training courses."

"Esther tells us you're looking after your sister? That's wonderful."

"Ah, thanks. It sort of fell on me to do it."

"And you like acting too, we noticed? Esther has always enjoyed drama."

"I'm not a great fan of acting," he said. "Joining that play was more about getting to know the suspects."

"The cast," Esther exclaimed. What was up with him? "We really loved getting to know the actors and, um, wanted to make some more friends who like acting, so they could help us improve."

Her mother eyed her, pulling her glasses down her nose. It made Esther feel like she was in the witness stand. But after a second, she changed tack. "Now, I told you we had a contact for you, Esther. Dennis and Sharon's nephew needs an assistant music teacher for a holiday programme at Upper Ledstow," her mum said. "The circumstances have changed and they need some help quickly. This could be perfect for you."

"But I'm not a music teacher," she said, already aware that it was probably a good opportunity.

"It's an *assistant* job. You need to broaden your net. In more ways than one," she added.

"What's that supposed to mean?"

"Nothing at all," her mother said, briskly. "I've got all the details here. Bernie Holland. I'll just ring through to him now while you're with me."

While her mother had a loud conversation, she hissed to Clark, "What are you doing?"

"Nothing."

"I said *ixnay on the urders may*." Hopefully, he'd understand Pig Latin.

"Oh right, sorry."

Her mother called over to her. "Esther, come out to the kitchen with me, please!"

Esther's stomach sank. She leaned against the bench.

Her mother turned around and pursed her lips, then stared at her for a long moment. She tucked her grey hair behind her ear. "Now, don't overreact. You know what my powers are, don't you? I believe I might have used them on Clark. I think he might have had his emotions removed. Temporarily, of course!"

Anger followed surprise as she realised what her mother had said. "You spelled my boyfriend! What the hell! This is a new low even for you."

"That's not fair. It was an accident," her mother said, calmly. "Honestly, I wanted to use it on myself. But I guess he was within hearing distance. I've been quite disappointed that you're too embarrassed of us to let me meet him. And I was talking to Margaret—"

"From the tennis club?" Esther put in.

"Yes, she's the Secretary of the committee. Been there for years."

"How did I guess?"

"Anyway, she said that sometimes when I get disappointed, I can get a bit snappy. I didn't want to act like that, if I could help it. I wanted to make a good impression because it seems like he is really important to you."

Esther breathed in through her nose. "Alright. What can you do about it? Tell me you can remove it."

Her mother pursed her lips. "Well, I haven't found a way to do that. But from past experience, it should wear off in about six to eight hours. Perhaps a bit sooner if you watch a sad movie?"

Esther massaged her temples. "Okay, right. We can deal with this."

"But Esther, there's something else. Are you getting involved in something? I'm only asking because in my line of work, I see people who try to subvert the natural process all the time. It's better to let the justice system handle it. It doesn't end well for those people."

She sighed. "Ledstow's the best place in the world, mum. It's welcoming to everyone and the community all pitches in when they need to. I'd never do anything to sabotage that. And Clark is with the police, remember." And that was how she stayed honest with her mother while not directly addressing the question at all.

"Come on, we're off," she said to Clark straight after that. Who knew what he might say to her parents next? If he had no shame, no embarrassment, no fear, he might blurt anything out.

"But I'm still hungry," he answered, adding extra roast potatoes flavoured with butter and rosemary to his plate. "These are good."

"Don't you have lots of work to do?" She said through her teeth. She raised her eyebrows at him but he wasn't taking the hint.

"Are you leaving so quickly?" Her mother asked, the

picture of innocence. "Well, Bernie is going to reach out to you tomorrow. So make sure you answer the phone."

"Yep, I will."

"And don't be late."

It was only once Clark had finished all of the food on his plate that he let her pull him out the door.

"Alright, I'll tell you why. My mother accidentally spelled you." She glanced at him from the corner of her eye as they walked down the steps.

"Oh. What spell?" His voice sounded only mildly interested. Esther guessed the spell must be working exactly as it should be. Normally he'd have the mad academic gleam in his eye right now.

"She's a judge, right? This spell is one that she has used on herself to take the emotion out of a situation, so that you can take a more objective view and make decisions based on the facts."

"She turned me into a detached judge? Well, that sounds relatively harmless." He got into the patrol car and put the key in the ignition.

"If you were at a cake competition, maybe. I'm worried you might not be so happy about it later on."

"I can think of a few things I'd like to judge you on," he said, one eyebrow raised. "Your cooking is what I meant! Cooking, jeez."

"Alright, fine," she replied. "I'll allow it."

"I thought you loved living in Ledstow?" she asked Clark the next morning. It had been bothering her that he didn't seem to be on the same page as her. She couldn't see herself ever living anywhere else.

He stretched his hands behind his head. "I guess I don't quite feel like I fit in here. In the police force, coming from out of town makes me different. You know Shona and Derek at work? They grew up here, along with most of the support staff. They know who the school librarian was in the 1970's and the best make-out spots in the hills for teenagers. They know the houses where dodgy deals happen and the perfect places to park in the summer when the tourists are visiting. And I'm not really a policeman so I don't feel I should put in the effort to learn all about these things. I'm just here to investigate paranormal phenomena."

"Why did you come here in the first place? I know you said you'd noticed paranormal activity here but was it really a lot more than other places?"

"I was getting a lot of reports from the region. I started mapping them and they seemed concentrated near here. Then I got a tip-off and came out for a field trip. At that time, the energy levels were off the charts. I told my supervisor and he arranged the job with the police. The levels have never been as high since then, though."

"When was that?"

"Last October."

"I wonder if it was around Halloween?"

He frowned. "Yes, I suppose it would have been."

"My grandmother says that the veil between worlds is thinner at certain times of year, letting the supernatural cross over into our world." Esther placed two coffee mugs on the table. Her grandmother, who she called 'nan', was more like a parent to her. She had always talked to her about the paranormal, even though she couldn't tell her anything about witchcraft.

"I have heard the folklore but I hadn't actually considered that as a factor."

"So are you only here for a year then? Finishing up in a few months?" They had spent so much time together in the last three months but had never discussed anything of the future.

He looked at her. "In theory, yes," he said, slowly.

"And then what?"

He placed his hand over hers, one finger stroking lightly over her skin. "Then we discuss together what the next steps are. I'm not just going to get on a train one day and leave."

"Hey, thanks for being so chilled about the spell," Esther said. "I can't believe my mother did that. There was never anything magical in the house for most of my childhood. No mention of it at all. Do you want breakfast?"

Clark shook his head. "I'll get something after my first meeting. I still think there must be another explanation for my behaviour yesterday." He grabbed his mug of black coffee and brought it to his lips, trying to drink it quickly even though it was scalding hot. "Perhaps it was just my mood or the situation? Maybe it was a stress response. Have you heard of the placebo effect?"

"Are you saying you don't believe in magic?" She eyed him carefully.

He took a large gulp of his drink, obviously forgetting about the temperature, and winced as the burning liquid went down his throat. "Magic? That's a very difficult question. I believe in observable and measurable effects that are outside normal ranges. I've seen enough of that, like dream telepathy and psychokinesis. Like how paranormal experiences often happen when the brain is relaxed." He gave a shrug. "But it's somehow different when it applies to me. And the cause of it can often be attributed to something other than what it's purported to be. I'm just not sure."

"Does my mother seem like someone who would believe in woo woo weird stuff?"

"No she doesn't, actually." He frowned.

"If there's one thing I've learned in the last few months, it's that if it looks like a pixie and walks like a pixie, it's a blooming pixie. But it's not up to me to convince you." He really was frustrating. He could believe that people could communicate with each other while dreaming but not that he'd been spelled by a music witch.

"I get it." He kissed her on the forehead. "I'm going to spend tonight at home. I need to spend some time with Triss to help her study. But I might see you for lunch?"

"I'll let you know how I'm going. I might have that interview today."

"Perfect. And good luck."

♫

IT WASN'T TOO long after that that her phone rang. She was getting dressed and had to hop from the bedroom to the lounge with one leg in her tights and the other leg of her tights bunched around her foot. "Must. Get to the phone," she grunted. "Am *not flaky*. Must answer phone. Hello?"

"Good morning. It's Bernie Holland here." He had a very posh accent that evoked leather, fine whiskey and bookcases.

"Hello. Thank you for reaching out."

"Not a problem. Er, you sound a little out of breath? Are you alright?"

Her eyes fell on Louis, who was staring at her as if she was a fish flapping around on the ground. "Just, ah, walking my cat. He needs the exercise." She poked her tongue out at the feline, who deliberately turned his back on her, raising his fluffy tail.

"Alright. I was wondering if you are able to come in and meet with me this morning? Look, I'm awfully sorry that it's such short notice. But I am in a pickle here."

"Oh, yes. I'm available."

"Let's say two hours from now? Eleven?"

"Perfect."

"You know where Upper Ledstow High is? Go right at the entrance then to the end of the corridor."

"I can do that. See you then." Esther pressed the red

telephone to end the call and put the phone down, breathing out slowly. Her weirdness didn't seem to put him off. She pulled up her tights properly and straightened her dress in front of the mirror. Perhaps things were looking up.

♫

IN THE EVENT, she almost turned up late. Louis got his paw stuck in her favourite woolly bobble jersey and didn't take kindly to her removing it. Jay took fright at the commotion and flew into the windowpane. He ricocheted off the glass and landed on the floor, stunned.

When Esther reached down to check on him, Louis took that as a sign to creep up on the bird and just about pounced on him.

"No! Bad," she said to the kitten, lifting the bird carefully onto the armchair. He soon shook himself off and fluffed his feathers off. She checked her phone. "Alright, I just about have time to get there. This is fine."

Her optimism didn't last for long when she arrived at the college. The place was an absolute catastrophe.

A young man with curly red hair beckoned her into one of the classrooms. He pointed to his phone to indicate he was on a call. "Esther? My granddad is in hospital so I've got to take this. I'm really sorry." He bustled out of the room, leaving Esther to the chaos.

That was Bernie? A student with scrappy facial hair? She'd expected someone at least four decades older and a top hat and cane wouldn't have gone astray. Esther walked further into the classroom. Some kids were sitting with their feet up, some were staring at their phones. She looked around for a seat on the edge some-where, trying to ignore the stares.

"What are you here for?" a young person asked. "Not trying to be rude."

"No, it's fine," she said. "I've got a meeting with your teacher in about ten minutes. I was a little early."

"Are you his girlfriend?"

"Or his mum," the other one laughed.

"Neither," she said, with a sigh. "I might be helping him out with looking after this class."

"Are you a teacher?"

"No, I'm not, actually."

"Well, what makes you think you can teach us?"

"Why would we want to learn more boring old songs anyway?"

"Yeah. We probably know more than you."

The noise level in the classroom was reaching fever pitch. How did a dozen young ones make so much noise? Esther could feel the frog jumping around inside that meant her anxiety wasn't far away.

Someone banged the cymbals together and she flinched. A young man picked up his acoustic guitar and pretended to do a rockstar strum, making huge circles with his arm.

Music, that was what she knew. "Can I?" Esther reached for the guitar. The young man reluctantly passed it over. It had been a few months since she'd even touched a guitar, since her chosen instrument was a ukulele, but, soon enough, the muscle memory in her fingers kicked in. She started off by plucking some notes, experimentally. The kids turned away, already losing interest.

"What are you playing?" someone asked.

That sounded a bit like... Hmm, yes. She put one leg up on the chair to hold the guitar and played the first verse of *Your Song*, a piece that had been covered many times, including the version made famous by Elton John. It was one that always made her feel happy.

She made a clear picture in her mind of a calm, azure sea and started singing softly. She didn't have to work to put emotion into the song. It came naturally when she performed music that spoke to her. The calm flowed through her and out to the room as she sang.

When she opened her eyes, there was complete silence. A clock ticked on the wall.

One girl had moved up next to her and was sitting

cross-legged by her feet. She gave a long sigh. "You're a proper singer, aren't you?" she asked.

"Thank you. I'm getting there," she answered, without a trace of irony. "I'm in a band with my friend. We're called Soulful."

"I'd love to have a voice like that." The girl peered out at her through long dark hair over her face.

She looked up to see that the teacher was standing just inside the door, looking impressed at her bringing the energy level down. He beckoned her over.

"That was the nurse on the phone," Bernie said to her, forehead creased with concern. "I'm really sorry but I need to go to the hospital now. It's become critical overnight. So instead of getting someone to help out, I'll need someone to take over the class. You're perfect for this, Esther. I can tell that already."

She gaped. "Was that whole thing some kind of a test?"

"No, it wasn't," he said. "But you teach them to play like that and we'll pay you anything you like. I'll email you a contract as soon as I can. Again, I'm really sorry about the change of plans. I meant to ease you into it."

"Well, thank you." She blinked. It would be a lot more work than she had expected. But really, it would be great experience and she needed the money.

"I have all of the lessons planned out already, so you

don't need to worry about that. Can you give me all your details? We'll run the checks."

"Sure. I, um, expected someone a little older from your voice."

"Ah, that's my classical voice training coming through. Do you have any other questions for me right now?"

A million questions crowded her mind but she could see that he wanted to leave. She wrote down her details while Bernie got the class working on transcribing a song into another key.

"I'm glad you're going to be teaching us," the girl who had moved to the front said. She fiddled with a lock of dark hair. "I'm Willow, by the way."

"Nice to meet you." Esther's eyes fell on a beaded bracelet around the girl's wrist.

Willow pulled her sleeve down over it, almost embarrassed.

"Just saying, I hope that you're stronger than you look. The substitute teachers never last long."

Esther watched the girl thoughtfully. "How long have you been playing for?"

"Since I was eight. It's quite easy for me. Playing music is really the only time when I don't feel like a failure."

"Sorry to hear that."

The girl shrugged.

Esther sat at the teacher's desk, reading the materials Bernie had set out for her, trying to ignore the noise. A few of the young people had pulled out their phones and some others were screwing up paper balls and aiming for the bin. She had read once that it's not enough to love what you're teaching. You have to love who you're teaching, too. Esther was determined to stick this one out.

♪

"You are looking at the new holiday music programme head teacher," she said, spreading her arms as she entered the office.

Clark smiled and lifted his glasses onto his head. "Well done. I knew they'd love you. But I thought it was an assistant position?"

"Funny story. We should go out for lunch to celebrate and I'll tell you about it."

He nodded. "Lunch is good. I've just been clearing out the desk here. Found some files from thirty years ago. I got a bit distracted reading them." He shrugged. "We need this desk free, since we're getting a new officer today."

"Well, that sounds good. Some help for you."

He shook his head. "The Avon and Somerset police

are sending someone across. They think we're over-whelmed with crime here in Ledstow."

"We did have two murders in two months!"

"Yes, but we caught the perps, though."

"And maybe a third one," she added, darkly. "How are you getting on with the investigation?"

There was a rap on the doorframe and Shona elbowed her way into the office.

"Clark, this is the new guy. He's come to us from Bristol."

"Simon Whalley, sir," he said. He had close-cropped hair and a face that looked like he was holding back a grin.

"Whalley? Nice to meet you." Clark stood up and shook his hand. "I was expecting you a bit later."

"I'll leave you to get him up to speed," Shona said. She turned on her heel and left the room.

"Ah, I'm sorry, she's a woman of few words. And I'm actually just on my way out for lunch," he said to the young guy. "Have a seat over there and..." He waved a hand at the general mess. "Perhaps get yourself sorted out with some stationery and equipment. You can help me go through all these files later."

"Right, sir."

"POOR GUY," Esther said, when they were seated around the corner in Lottie's café. The smell of coffee and the comforting buzz of people surrounded them. The café was decorated in hanging ribbons and tiny butterflies that she thought must have been for the spring festival.

Clark shook his head. "Look, if they're going to keep an eye on us, they could at least do their homework first. That's exactly what they're doing, by the way. I'm not giving up lunch with a beautiful woman for some young upstart. Tell me how the interview went," he said, reaching for her hand.

"Bernie turned out to be young! I think he would have employed anyone at that moment. He'd just found out a family member was really sick and he needed someone to take over the job. I was there, I guess. It's only two weeks' work anyway."

"It will be good experience, though. And you do have the qualifications. Don't sell yourself short."

"Yeah, I do." A flush of pride spread through her. There was no reason to feel like an imposter. She hadn't tricked anyone into giving her a job, after all.

Lottie, resident witch and supplier of top-notch coffee, magical cakes, and gossip, arrived at the table, a broad grin on her face. She had a dish towel over her shoulder and a black apron tied over bright pink clothing. "Hello lovebirds. We have got two bagels with cream cheese and salmon here. The bagels were baked by yours truly this morning at sparrow's fart. I'm told they are sublime."

"Thank you."

She winked at them and returned to the kitchen.

Clark picked up his bagel and took a bite. "You asked about the case before? Well, it is getting more interesting by the day. Georgia's partner is in Paris at the moment. His flatmate has confirmed it. He's away for work and has been for the last week."

"He's in Paris? That's either really convenient or it means he definitely didn't do it."

Clark nodded.

"What about the funeral?"

He chewed and swallowed before answering. "We're having trouble getting hold of him but I assume he will be going to the funeral. Her parents said that they have messaged him. I'll get him down to the station for a chat when he gets here."

Esther bit into her bagel and rolled her eyes in delight. It was so fresh and fluffy with a little crunch from a light toasting.

"So good. What's next, then?"

"In my opinion, it looks suspicious, but we don't really have any leads yet. Might have been a random attack."

"Except for Jeremiah," she said.

"The boss?"

She nodded. "The barkeep. I never told you about that, did I?"

After Esther had told him about the argument she saw on the night of the talent quest, she added the gossip the two old ladies had told her.

"Hmm. So you think that Georgia might have been sleeping with him? That adds extra motive for both Ravi, as the boyfriend, and Jeremiah, as the jealous lover."

"Yeah. Why not?"

"We can't assume anything just based on some gossip. And I can't even get to it for a few days. I've got paperwork coming out of my ears with bringing this new guy in at work as well."

"I can go and chat to Jeremiah some time tomorrow," Esther offered. "He rang Ashton yesterday saying we had left our spare microphone there from the talent quest."

Clark let out a sigh. "If I thought you'd listen, I'd say to wait until I can come with you. But…"

"You know me too well?"

He placed his hand over hers on the table and gave it a squeeze. "I know you too well."

CHAPTER 6

The next morning, Esther arrived at the college bright and early. She located the staff room and made herself a large cup of coffee with just a splash of milk. Soon enough, all of the young people trickled into the classroom, bringing a hubbub of noise.

"Morning, everyone. I'm Esther. My favourite things are musicals and my pets. But enough about me. I'd like everyone to go round and do a quick introduction." Someone groaned. "Yeah, I know. Normally I'd be the last one to want to take part in one of these." She racked her brain for a way to make it a little different, drumming her fingers on the desk. "Why don't you tell me your name and which song describes your life?"

"Boring," said one of the boys.

"I'll go first," she continued, smoothly, as if he hadn't spoken. "Mine is *Fight Song* by Rachel Platten."

A kid who looked about nine started singing *Pony,* showing off teeth with braces. There was a collective sigh and some people rolled their eyes.

After a short pause, someone spoke up. "*So What* by Pink. My parents are splitting up." The girl lifted her chin as if daring Esther to tell her it wasn't true.

"I'm really sorry to hear that. What's your name?"

"Izzy."

Another young man spoke softly. "I'm Arthur. I don't know a song for it but I'm going to move away soon. Not my choice. Stepdad is forcing us to move." The young man looked down at his table and folded his arms.

"Thank you, Arthur." It seemed as if they were trying to outdo each other. At least they were engaging with her, she supposed.

"*Say My Name* from Beetlejuice," the girl called Willow said. She was wearing an elaborate woven hairband today.

"Oh, do we have another fan of musicals? Great."

"Something like that." She nudged the person next to her.

"Does anyone else want to go?" After a few people had mumbled their way through their introductions, Esther wrapped it up. "First we're going to do some scales. Do you all know how to do those?" There were a few nods. Most people didn't seem to be listening. "What I want you all to focus on is doing them in time. When I clap, that'll be the first beat. We'll keep it to four four time. Pick up your instruments. Ready?"

She brought her hands together and a few of the kids started playing.

"Here. Izzy, was it? Bring your hand further around." She got up to help the girl with her hand position.

As she came back, she noticed that Willow was missing from her seat and stuck her head out the door. The corridor was cold and gloomy and the lockers on either side made it feel ominous. The only light came from a window at the end of the row.

"Willow?" she called, walking a few steps down the hallway. "Are you out here?"

Curls of smoke rose from the ground and disappeared into the gloom. Smoking in the hallway, huh? Some things never changed.

"Come on, Willow," Esther said, louder this time. "Back into class."

"Oh, I didn't hear you," the girl said, scrambling up from the floor between two rows of lockers.

"You know, you can do whatever you're doing at lunchtime," Esther added, as they walked back down the hallway.

"What? No, I don't need to," Willow stammered. "Sometimes, I just have to get out of the classroom. It gets too loud."

Esther held the door open for her. She knew that feeling herself, and the noise level seemed to have tripled in the five minutes since she'd left.

"Alright. Just let me know first next time." She smiled at Willow, who drifted back towards her chair.

So she had to keep tabs on all these kids individually, while making sure they learned something? Esther really felt like she was out of her depth here. Wasn't there a retired teacher somewhere who would do a better job at this?

She shook her head. Back to the scales. This was basic stuff but it did require the kids to listen and co-operate with each other. They had five hours left in the day to get it right. "Okay, everyone. Let's try this again. From the top."

AFTER SCHOOL, Esther walked around the corner to the pub. The Twig and Berries was feeling extra empty today. The squishy seats were depressed, the fire was out and some of the chairs were half pulled out from the table, as if people had left in a hurry. Normally, the afternoon crowd would be just settling in with a pint about now.

Jeremiah pulled out the spare microphone and put it on the bar when he saw her come in. "Hello there."

She came up to the bar. "Thank you. But how did you know it belonged to us? I know that it's ours from this little scratch right here on the handle." Picking it up, she turned it to show him.

"It's my super power," he said, laughing. "Do you know how many lost jackets, phones and wallets I get in here?"

"I can imagine it's quite a few."

"I've always known who left things at our house, even as a kid. My old man just thought it was funny. It was a party trick to him."

Jeremiah bent down and brought out a bowl of crisps, which he set on the bar leaner between them.

Esther smiled briefly. She was wondering how to broach the topic of his deceased employee and decided the direct approach was the best option. "Hey, it's absolutely awful about Georgia. She always seemed really nice. I was so, so sorry to hear about that."

"Oh, thanks."

"And just after she won the talent quest too!"

"Yeah, I really hope the police find out what happened. It won't bring her back, though, of course. Gone far too young." Jeremiah lapsed into silence.

"What was she like to work with? Did you get on well with her?"

He nodded. "She wasn't the best employee I've had but I didn't talk down to her, just gave it to her straight. She appreciated that, I think."

"It's going to be hard for a while, isn't it?"

"The funeral is the first thing. And Merrin can't even come."

"Oh! Who's Merrin?"

"My partner. We're in a long-distance relationship. It works fine, mostly. It's just times like this that stretch both of us."

It took a minute for Esther's brain to catch up. She'd already spun out the scenario that Georgia's partner had found out about Jeremiah in her mind. "If you're with Merrin…"

His eyebrows shot up. "What?"

"The two old women that live next door said they'd seen you and Georgia looking nice and cosy. They thought you might be, er, an item."

Jeremiah breathed out through his nose. "Those old gossips! No, it's actually far stranger than that. She was like my little sister."

"You can tell me." Esther jumped onto the barstool, letting him know that she wasn't going anywhere until she got the truth. "It doesn't seem like you're too busy, right now."

Jeremiah narrowed his eyes at her. "I'm not, it's true. It all started as a favour, probably three years ago now. I was meant to be teaching her cocktail making. But, in a twist that shocked both of us, it turned out that I was teaching her magic."

"Alright. Go on."

"You're not laughing."

"You haven't said anything funny," she responded. It almost seemed like there were more magical beings in Ledstow than nonmagical people - all pretending they weren't magical and everything was normal. It was like a huge game of 'I know something you don't know' or a battle of wits. "I've often thought that there was something special about the way that you know what people want to eat before they do."

"Well, I was talking to her mum. Harriet and I go way back. She was worried about her daughter as Georgia had started getting into a bit of trouble. So I offered to take her on in the bar to give her something to do.

She learnt very quickly but was always looking for the next thrill. I could tell as I was like that when I was young too. And I realised that she was using magic, so I very carefully began giving her tips without letting on that I knew. I didn't want to put her off. But I told her about it eventually." He picked up a glass and automatically began polishing it with a tea towel.

"So you were the one who told her that she had magical powers?"

He nodded. "She was just starting to really get it. She was so good."

"What did you fight about? I saw you that night. The night of the talent quest. You looked really angry with her."

He clicked his tongue. "What you have to realize about her is that she didn't listen. To anyone. Ever." He paced a few steps, waving the glass around. "I think she might have had the capacity to be strong. Like really strong. She was a fire mage but she didn't control it. That day, she flicked her fingers and the gas in the kitchen caught. She was frustrated at a customer and impulsively cast. I had to make a big deal of it in front of the other staff so that they didn't catch on. Talking about kitchen safety and risk and all of that stuff. So I was a little upset with her but not angry."

"Mm, alright." Esther could empathise with the lack of control.

"It wasn't the first time, either. Her parents had pretty much given up on her."

"That's awful. So she couldn't control her magic?"

"No, she didn't *want* to control it. She thought it would be more powerful if she used untamed magic. Just quietly, I think her dad was pretty ruthless. She often complained that he was really strict and still treated her like a little kid."

"And what time did she leave here that night?"

"After the talent show, most people left pretty quickly. I think she only stayed to help clear the glasses and have a celebratory drink. Then I said she could go."

"So would you say that was about nine thirty?"

"Oh, it wouldn't have taken quite that long. Nine, maybe? I told her I would be fine by myself for the rest of the night as she seemed keen to go."

Keen to go? After she'd just won the contest?

"Thanks, Jeremiah. See you soon."

"Do you want anything before you go?"

Although she hated to decline when he obviously needed customers, she'd had a long day. "Sorry, not today. We'll be in some time this week, though."

She waited until she got around the corner before getting her phone out to ring through to Clark. "I just went to see Jeremiah at the pub. We have another case that's not exactly straight forward."

"What do you mean?" He sounded resigned. "I'm already planning to go door to door on Thursday after-noon to find any witnesses."

"I should be able to join you after I've finished at school. Get this: You're going to need your trusty partner again. It turns out Georgia was magical."

CHAPTER 7

Esther held up crossed fingers. "Lucky last."

She and Clark were visiting the properties that backed onto the part of the park where the crime scene was. The cloudy day mirrored their moods after a long afternoon of people who saw nothing, heard nothing, and otherwise were precisely no help to them.

"In a town full of busybodies, how can nobody know anything?" Clark asked, with a sigh. "Let's finish off a long and fruitless afternoon by visiting this one last place."

"It wasn't entirely fruitless. We got banana cake as well as enough cups of tea to sink a ship. Surely those count as fruit? And we suffered through some gossip about the librarian, survived looking at old Mr Martin's stamps, and narrowly escaped having to help at the upcoming cake stall."

He threw her a look as they knocked on the door of a small flat at the very end of the row.

When the door opened, Clark smiled and put out a hand. "Ledstow police. We're investigating a crime in the area. We're here to ask whether you saw or heard anything on Sunday night.

The young woman shrugged. "I didn't see nothing." She moved her baby to the other hip and it reached chubby fingers towards a chunk of her hair.

"Are you sure? It's important."

"Ouch! I was probably doing my yoga online at that time. It's my only time to myself, really." Her glance fell on her other son, who was outside the glass door to the garden. "But Mason was probably outside for some of that time. No matter what I do, he finds his way out into the garden. He's eaten more dirt than sausages, I swear."

"Could we have a quick chat to him?"

"Yeah."

The house smelt like a rich casserole and Esther's stomach gurgled in response. The woman opened the door to the tiny garden and stood beside the doorway as they crossed the patio.

"Hi, Mason," Esther said.

"Hello. This is Jeanie," he said, going up a plastic

ramp and perching precariously on the top. He held up a figurine.

"Superman," Esther said, smiling.

"Nah. I call him Jeanie, because mum said he wears his undies outside his jeans."

"We just want to ask you about Sunday night, if that's alright."

In response, the boy flew the figurine around in a circle making a whooshing noise. "He's in a team. It is the three of us fighting crime. I'm super fast. I have to be because Cleary only helps us sometimes." He dipped the toy down low.

Clark squatted down. "Could you answer us, son? This would be a way that you could help us to fight some real crime right here in town. We just want to know if you heard or saw anything the other night."

"You're crime fighters? Mum says policemen get paid for sitting on their bottoms," he said, still playing with his toys.

Esther smothered a laugh but didn't dare to look at Clark's face. "Bless."

"Cleary would probably know. He's really tough. Even Jeanie and me can't beat him."

Clark wandered over to the stone wall backing onto the park and peered over the top.

"This is another toy? And what does Cleary look like?" she asked, sitting down on the ground. It was a cool afternoon and the chill of the patio seeped through her clothes. Everything looked and felt different from down here.

"He's a squirrel. But he changes."

"That's pretty cool. What does he look like now?"

"He's not here right now. But he's like a chameleon. If he's on the grass, he's grass coloured."

"I wish I could do that."

"Me too," Mason replied quickly. "He only comes when he's scared. And he always does the same thing. He's really funny."

"I've just remembered something," his mother said, coming out and pulling her cropped sweatshirt down against the chill. "I saw Mason sitting up on the wall talking to Father P," she said. "I remember because I came out and waved to him."

"Father Pedro?" Clark asked. "Ah. Thank you. That's really helpful."

"He's got a great imagination, doesn't he?" She asked the woman as they walked back inside.

"Yeah, he told me once that his invisible friend was dead."

"Oh." A shiver ran up Esther's spine.

"Kids, huh?"

When they went outside, she said, "I thought I was getting somewhere with him. And who's Father Pedro?"

"He's the one who called in the body. But we

thought he couldn't speak English very well. He pretty much refused to tell us anything." He checked something on his phone. "Looks like he lives just over here. But it will have to be tomorrow. It's almost dinner time."

CHAPTER 8

"Why on earth didn't you question him further at the time?" Esther asked, exasperated, as they got out of the car in front of the priest's house. "Of course a priest would have to be able to speak English."

"I knew that he had been a priest at one point, maybe a long time ago when he was in Spain. I didn't know he was still a priest now."

"I keep forgetting you're new to town. We have three priests here in Ledstow."

The door was opened by a cheerful man with a slim build in a polo shirt and slacks.

Clark stepped forward. "Nice to meet you, Father. As I said on my call, we are investigating the death of

Georgia Haddock," he said, shaking hands with the smiling man. The priest placed his other hand over the top in a small but reassuring gesture which seemed to show that he was listening. They were led into a comfortable house. Someone was listening to opera music down the hallway. "I'm Detective Clark. And this is Esther Forte."

"Come in, come in. And you can call me Pedro," he said, in his lightly accented English, removing his cap and going into the kitchen. "Forgive me, I've just been out in the garden, pruning the roses and getting the beds ready for planting. But I'll make us a cup of tea." He moved about the kitchen, whistling and talking, while they looked over the garden. "Terrible circumstances. Terrible. So you think it might not be natural causes?"

"Do you remember what you were doing at the time?" Clark asked, impatient.

"Sunday the third of April, you said?"

"Yes. Around nine thirty p.m."

He brought a tray with a teapot, a jug of milk, and three cups and saucers, over to the small table. Then he sat down and looked at both of them in turn.

"You were the one who alerted the police?" Esther asked, feeling like the priest could tell more about her than she could about him.

He nodded. "I was over in the park. I called up and told them about it."

"Why didn't you say much the other night?" Clark asked.

"I'm sorry." He actually looked a little guilty.

"Can you tell me what you saw that night?" Esther asked.

The man pressed his lips together in a line and shook his head. Clark folded his arms.

"Alright. Why not?"

"Perhaps it would be judicious to ask in which activity I was occupied at the particular time." Pedro steepled his fingers and stared at her calmly.

She stared back. "Sure. What were you doing?"

"I was getting a plane out of a tree for a little boy that lives next door."

"Who?"

Clark sat back with his arms crossed, watching the interplay.

"His name's Mason. The boys and their mother do their best, but I like to help them out when I can."

"We met him. He seems like an imaginative young kid."

"Oh, he is."

"So you saw something at that time?"

"I haven't figured out how to process it yet. I need to ask God what the meaning of it is. I'm simply not ready to disseminate all the details with anyone except for Him."

"Okay, I can understand that. When do you think you'll be ready?" she asked, ignoring the huffing sound that was coming from Clark.

"Spiritual conversations don't happen via text messages," he said. "Patience. I will get in touch with you when the time is right."

"Alright. I'll look forward to it." Esther stood up and reached for her empty cup to put it in the kitchen but the priest motioned to leave it.

"I'll deal with it."

"We'll leave it there for today, then. Thanks for your help," Clark said, leading the way to the door. Just as he opened it, there was a call from behind them.

"Oh, Miss Forte?" he called. "I knew her, you know. Georgia. She came to me for counsel."

"She did? I know you probably can't share much about it, but I'd love to know more. Anything that could help me — I mean, us — to figure out exactly what happened."

Pedro came closer, speaking softly. "She was… stressed. Her parents were going to throw her out, so her mum asked if I could help. In the end, her job at the bar was the best thing for her. But I fear she was in some… trouble."

"What sort of trouble?"

"I'm not sure. It's only that she didn't have as much time for our chats. She was very driven when she wanted to be. She must have recently moved in with her partner, Ravi, in the last month. Or she planned to. I get the feeling he was maybe more keen than her."

"Mm," she said. "That's helpful." The police had already checked and Ravi was out of town on the night of the crime. Perhaps it would be worth double-checking his alibi.

"I told you that it would be a waste of time," Clark said, as they went out the door. "Why do I feel like we've just had a moral lesson on patience?"

"I don't think it's a waste of time when you're getting to know people. And don't you feel like he's got the measure of us?"

"Yes. He seemed to like you, though."

Esther didn't say that was probably because she was a little more patient than him. "We should probably talk more to Georgia's parents. They must know more than they are letting on."

THAT EVENING, Esther video-called with her grandmother, who was in bed with the after-effects of a virus. Hope's face was paler than normal, her hair undyed and white against the pillow.

"It's lovely to be able to talk with you, sweetheart," Hope said. "And good of the nurse to set it up for me."

"You too, nan. Are you feeling any better?"

"Oh, yes. A little better."

"I've been missing our witchy chats."

"Oh, me too. Although Kevin has come every day this week to do the crossword with me."

"He's a good friend."

"I offered to tell his fortune in the tea leaves and I think I put him off." She laughed.

"Have I told you that there's been a suspected murder here in town?"

"Another one?"

"You know how we came second in the talent quest? It was the woman who won it. Her name was Georgia and she worked at the pub."

"Oh, how awful," her grandmother said. "And you're investigating it, I suppose?"

"Yeah, she had magic powers so I'm helping Clark out with it."

"Be careful, Blue Eyes. Make sure you know what you're getting yourself into."

"I will. We've got a priest keeping secrets, a partner in Paris, and not a whole lot else at the moment."

"It will all come out in the wash," Hope said, comfortably. "My tip for today is if you want to start feeling the energies around you, you could try looking at the symbols in your life; recurring themes, shapes, things, motifs in your dreams. Then look up what they mean. That's how we become more attuned to the messages the universe is giving us."

"I'll try," she answered. "But sometimes I think the universe is a little confused."

CHAPTER 9

The Haddocks lived in a large townhouse down a long driveway right next to the library. Esther eyed the immaculate front garden and tidy but dated house.

"Hello again, Mr and Mrs Haddock," Clark said. "This is Esther."

"Sir," the man said, holding out a hand. He held himself straight as a rod, and even if Esther didn't know he was ex-military, she would suspect it on seeing him. "Madam."

"Hello."

"Harriet," he almost barked into a doorway on the way down the hall. Esther peeked in as she trailed behind the other two.

The woman was sitting on an office chair in a tiny

room. Laid out on the table was a mass of pins and string and she was passing wooden handles one over the other with the accuracy of a sushi chef.

"Oh, I'm sorry." The woman looked over her shoulder at Esther. "I get stuck into this and then it's really hard to come back to the real world."

She stepped inside the room, "That's what I'm like with music. But that looks really complicated."

"It's lace making. I know it looks confusing but it isn't really. I believe someone has to keep these old traditions alive. I even sell some things online."

The woman got up and Esther followed her out to the sitting room, which was sparsely decorated in shades of brown. "Would you like something to drink? Brian?"

While the woman busied herself getting cups of tea and a bottle of water for her husband, Esther sat on one end of the couch.

"How can we assist this time? You've already asked us if we knew anything. We told you that we don't know much about her life now."

"Did she still live here?"

"Oh, when she wanted to."

Harriet brought out the drinks and set them on the coffee table, looking worriedly out the window. A few moments later, she got up again and started fiddling with some of the greeting cards on the side table.

"Sit down, for Pete's sake."

"I can't, Brian. I'll get some afternoon tea." She got up and went into the kitchen, where she stood, shuffling the cards while not looking at them. Esther felt sorry for her as a grieving mother.

"We really need you to tell us if you can remember her mentioning anything strange or anything that she was worried about."

"Superstitious claptrap," he barked. "That's what she worried about."

"I'm just making sure I've covered everything. You two weren't at the talent quest?"

"No. She didn't tell us about it."

"And you didn't see her afterwards?"

While Clark talked to Mr Haddock, Esther stood up to help Harriet, who had paused, with a packet of biscuits in her hand, staring into the sink.

"Would you like me to take those?"

"Thanks. I was going to serve them on a plate. What do you even do with these? Keep them?" 'These' were a bouquet of flowers that were turning brown and wilted. "She hardly even looked at them."

"You could dry them by hanging them upside down," Esther offered. "Do you know who they were from?"

"They arrived that morning. I assume they were from her boyfriend, Ravi. He liked to spoil her. When they were together, that is. Sometimes they were off, sometimes they were on."

"Just tie some string to them like this and hang them up somewhere."

"Alright. I'll hang them in my craft room. Brian never goes in there."

"It'll be nice to keep them."

Harriet leaned against the bench. "Oh, I'm dreading tomorrow. It's the funeral and I feel like the whole family blames me."

"Don't be so silly, Harriet," Brian called from the other room.

She lowered her voice. "I was too permissive with her. That's what they think, anyway."

"You can get through tomorrow," Esther said. "Everyone will be thinking about Georgia, not casting blame."

"Will you come with me?" When Esther looked surprised, Harriet laughed. "I'm sorry, I know it seems ridiculous. But I need one person there who isn't going to judge me."

"I get that." She thought for a moment. It might be a good way to find some more people who might know what was going on in Georgia's life. "Alright, I'll do my best to come along."

♪

"I MIGHT HAVE AGREED to go to the funeral tomorrow, as a support person," she told Clark when they got into his car.

"That works out well." He started up the car. "I found Brian Haddock generally quite an unhelpful person, though he did say that Ravi may not have replied to their messages as they didn't always get on well."

"Right." She pulled her phone out. "Oh, I've got a voicemail message."

It was Father Pedro. "Hello, Esther. I've spoken at length with Him. I'm ready to talk to you but it has to be on the first of the month. Come over to my place. I'll see you then. It might not even help but I have to be satisfied with myself that I've told you whatever I can."

He wanted to meet with her on the first? That was just under three weeks away. Esther put it to the back of her mind. She had a lot to think about before that.

"Everything ok?" Clark pulled her out of her thoughts.

"Yeah, just sometimes these investigations are painfully slow."

"I've got one case I've been chasing for months. It's glacial. Hey, you know I've mentioned my supervisor at the university before?"

"Vaguely."

"The Head of Department is what you'd imagine if

you had to think of a dragon trapped in a human's body, right down to the snorting. He's a grumpy old fart."

She laughed. "Sounds delightful."

"He's called me back to the university."

"Oh! You have to go back? For how long?"

"I've booked a flight for tomorrow. It should only be a few days, as long as I can convince him that he doesn't need me. I just really don't want to annoy him, as he's been making noises about retiring soon."

"And would you be in line for his job?"

"Potentially."

"But how can you leave now? What about the murder investigation?"

"Shona's there. And the young lad, Simon."

"So you're saying it'll be on hold until you get back?"

He gave her a look.

"I think they'll do what they can, but yes, the investigation will be on hold. The most frustrating part about it is that I was going to catch Ravi when he came back for the funeral. That's tomorrow."

$\mathcal{E}$sther did not want to be here. However, she had promised Mrs Haddock that she would come and Esther Forte did not break her promises - unless endometriosis, anxiety, or sometimes witchcraft, caused her to break them, of course. She didn't voluntarily break promises, anyway.

After asking Bernie Holland for the day off the music programme, she got dressed in her best clothes and came down to the Sacred Heart Church on this wet afternoon.

It felt strange to be surrounded by Georgia's family and friends, who were all dressed in various shades of navy, grey and black. Harriet mostly ignored her, her hands clasped in another woman's, who looked like she could be a sister, from her similar brown, lightly-curled hair and snub nose. At least her family wasn't ignoring Harriet, as she had feared.

Esther was in the front row on the left side, with the family, but she had at least claimed a spot at the very edge, giving her a good place to observe the guests.

Jeremiah was dressed in a huge black coat and purple scarf. Esther wasn't used to seeing him out of the setting of his pub. He nodded to Mr Haddock, who went over and shook his hand in greeting. That made sense as they knew each other well.

Ravi, a clean-cut man with dark hair and light-brown skin, sank into a chair in the corner. Esther recognised him from the picture Clark had shown her.

Iris Grey came in, helped by Cara, the librarian, who gave Esther a nod. Iris was the elder witch of the village coven. She sat down slowly, next to Ravi in the back row. He didn't appear to know the old woman as he stared down at his phone. It was also interesting that he didn't sit with Georgia's parents.

Small towns were as intricate as the lace that Mrs Haddock made; each person a thread wound around the others to make up a larger pattern. Sometimes it was beautiful. Sometimes, not. But everybody's fate relied, to some extent, on their neighbours.

"How did you know her?" a man asked, interrupting her thoughts. It was Hamish Falkirk, the bearded musician. *Hide your Tamagotchi*, she thought to herself.

"Oh, I'm really here as a support person. You?"

"Distant cousin."

"Oh. So you went up against your family in the contest the other night?"

He looked at her strangely. "Yeah, I guess I did. You were there?"

She nodded. "I'm in the band Soulful."

A slow smile of recognition spread across his face. "Oh yeah. You sang *Fast Car*. That was good."

"Is Iris in the family as well?"

"I'm not sure." He looked off to the side, obviously wanting to cut the conversation short.

"Alright." Her intuition twitched at everything this guy said. She wanted to talk to him further but he didn't seem to be interested in a long conversation.

Father Pedro walked up the front and everyone took their seats. He gave a short but heartfelt introduction. Esther could see his father, Bernardo, sitting to the right side too.

Georgia's father stood up next. He spoke in bursts and kept one hand in his pocket.

"Morning, everyone. I'm Brian Haddock, Georgia's father. I don't know half of you who are here today, although you've probably heard of me. We didn't get on that well in the last few years." He swallowed hard. "I was trying."

"That's alright," Pedro reached a hand out to him.

"Georgia was fiercely independent. I was proud of her perseverance with training. But we hardly found any photos of her older than about twelve. She was very good at dodging away when a camera was near."

A series of photos were projected onto the wall. Georgia in a sandpit. Georgia finishing a race. Georgia in a pool with steam rising up around her.

"She'd get in the pool at any time of year," her father said. "Even in the depths of winter."

The final one was much more recent. Georgia must have been around eighteen. She was smiling and tucking her hair behind her ear. Her wrist was covered in a blue beaded bracelet that reminded Esther of something but she couldn't quite grasp it.

"It's time to pay your respects if you wish," Pedro said, shortly.

Mrs Haddock, draped liberally in a black lace dress that Esther guessed was handmade, stepped up to the side of the coffin and reached a finger out to lightly touch the wooden surface. Father Pedro rested a hand on her shoulder and murmured some words to her. Esther looked for Mr Haddock, who was to be found rocking on the balls of his feet, hands in his pockets, staring out the church door at the rain. She could see why poor Harriet needed moral support and went over to her.

Ham Falkirk and a woman who looked like his

mother stood beside them silently. Esther watched with interest as they crossed themselves and turned away.

The town florist, Nell, wiped something from her cheek. She was tall with a slim build and always moved with a certain grace. Esther wondered if she had once been a ballet dancer. Nell leaned down to straighten the floral arrangement, looking around her rather guiltily.

She couldn't help but think that funerals tried to be everything to everyone. But that wasn't how people worked. You couldn't capture everything a person was with a few words and some sandwiches. It was preposterous.

Take Esther herself, for example. To her parents, a daughter. To her boss, an employee. To Ash, a band-mate. To her cat, an annoying house servant. Each of these saw a slightly different side of her.

It seemed that Georgia had even more pronounced differences in her personality depending on who she was with. Now that she was gone, she only existed as different versions in peoples' memories, almost like a puzzle that the people in her life were trying to re-create.

A flash of gold caught her eye and she noticed three shady looking guys in hooded coats who had come in during the service and were standing in the back corner. One had a large gold watch wrapped around his pale wrist. A shiver ran across her shoulders when one looked her way but they didn't make any further moves, standing silently, looking around them.

Jeremiah clapped his hands a few times to get attention. "Alright folks, make your way slowly to the pub and we'll have a wee bite and a drop for Georgia. Those of you who want to are welcome to join us."

He moved towards the coffin as if to say something to Mrs Haddock, but it was then that the poor lady let out a scream and her hand flew to her heart. Everyone else stepped back from the coffin and Esther saw what they had seen. Smoke hissed out and curled around the sides of the coffin, spiraling into the air.

"SOMEONE'S TRYING to give us a scare, that's for sure," Mrs Haddock said, once she was safely ensconced in an armchair in the pub, half-drunk whiskey in hand.

Most had quickly left the church following the scare, as they realised that the coffin wasn't on fire, until Esther, the Haddocks, Pedro, and his father were the only ones left. They had clumped into a group, casting suspicious glances at the coffin every now and then, but the smoke seemed to have vanished as quickly as it came.

"Terrible goings on," Pedro said, throwing a dark look at Brian Haddock.

Mr Haddock did peek under the coffin lid when urged to by his wife. But he stood up again quickly and came back to the group. "You and your ridiculous ideas, Harriet. Of course nothing's wrong. Never thought otherwise."

They unanimously decided that a strong tipple was exactly what was needed and walked in twos and threes to the pub on the next block.

Esther had somehow ended up walking next to Mr Haddock, with his wife on the other side of him. "Might as well have a sandwich and an old fashioned since I'm paying for it," Mr Haddock said. "They cost a lot, these things."

"Oh, do be quiet, Brian," Mrs Haddock said, and Esther tended to agree.

No one had said anything much until they got inside and their tongues seemed to thaw as well as their fingers. Esther ordered a glass of wine and sat on the couch next to Mrs Haddock. It was Jeremiah who started them off once they were all sufficiently hydrated.

"I've got a story for you," he began, waving his beer bottle around. "This was the Georgia I knew. Once, we had a function booked and I realized I had forgotten to get the fish for one of the set menu options. People were already arriving by that time; they were businessmen in suits and they looked impatient. I apologised to her but I had to run out to the market. When I got back, I expected it to be absolute chaos. But Georgia had provided free fries to them all and they were quite content. I found her in the middle of a thrilling checkers finale; it was her versus the boss. The others were either glued to the match or satisfied with their drinks and fries. She was having a great time, too."

"Ooh," said Mrs Haddock, but whether it was in shock or admiration, Esther wasn't sure.

"I taught her to play that," Brian said, but he trailed off as everyone ignored him.

"Another time, she broke up a fight in the carpark here by doing an impromptu fire juggling performance. And once, she forgot to lock the door when she left the pub so she went back at three in the morning to do it."

This time, Mrs Haddock gasped.

"By herself?"

"I do remember that. She didn't even wake me up," Ravi put in. "Just told me about it the next day."

"She could look after herself," Jeremiah agreed.

The unspoken words hung in the air. *Not in the end, she couldn't.*

Father Pedro cleared his throat. "Um. Not to bring the remembrances to a premature end but I think we should consider who might have wanted to disrupt the funeral."

After a brief silence, everyone started talking at once. Esther drifted off from the noise.

Ravi was standing at the bar, looking very alone, while everyone else chatted in small groups. He was very tall, with dark skin, and black hair in a stylish cut.

"Hi Ravi, I'm Esther. Would you be willing to have a little chat after this? About Georgia?"

"This is hardly the time," he said.

"I know. I'm really sorry about that. We've been trying to get in contact with you."

"I've been away."

"Yes, I know."

He tapped his fingers on the bar. "Are you a journalist or something? I have a lot of work to catch up on. So…"

"No, I'm not with the press. I'm helping with the investigation. Would you be able to contact me when you're free?"

He looked at her for the first time. "I don't think so. I don't air my personal issues with people I don't know."

She suppressed a sigh. She would probably react the same if she was in his position. "Alright, I'm sorry for bothering you, Ravi. Truly."

CHAPTER 11

$\mathcal{E}$sther woke, sweating, from a dream where she was being chased. A hooded figure pursued her through the hill trails of the gorge behind town. She knew it was getting closer but each time she turned around, the hooded figure turned around too. There was a symbol on the back of the hood that burned itself into the back of her eyelids. It was a grey shape with a perfectly circular hole in it, sort of like a fried egg without the yolk.

She reached for her phone to see that Clark had called twice, while the ringer was off. She called him back. He had been gone for a few days, already, but Esther's days were full with teaching. By the evening, she was shattered. Nothing new had come up in the investigation, and even if it had, she didn't have the brain space to deal with it.

"Some news this morning."

"Good morning to you, too," she said. "I'm feeling alright, thanks."

"Good morning," he said. It turns out that she was poisoned. "Conium maculatum. Commonly known as hemlock. But what the pathologist noticed was that the dose was very specific."

"That's awful!"

"It is. She was given just enough to survive for half an hour before she died."

"Okay, well we've got Ravi who is a pharmacist," she said. "But he was out of town. And he's not as bad as everyone said. I actually feel quite sorry for him."

Clark smiled grimly. "Might be time to check on that alibi."

"Crotchets!" She felt the colour drain from her face. "Father Pedro is a gardener, remember? He would know all about different plants and their properties."

Clark shook his head. "No, it can't be. There must be someone else. He was with his dad, anyway."

"What about the florist?"

"All good ideas."

"But what did you mean about the dose being very specific?"

"Well, the pathologist said that, in other cases that he's seen of poisoning, the dose was way too much.

Poison is usually the weapon of a crime of passion and it is usually favoured by a woman, in general. So the wife might throw in a large slug of poison to make sure the deed was done, if you like. But this time, the dose was exactly the right amount to make sure that the person died after a certain period of time."

"Right." That did point to Ravi, as a pharmacist. Jeremiah's cocktail making floated through her mind as well. She'd seen his exacting skill with glasses and bottles. But there was also Harriet, Georgia's mother, who was precise and perfectionist in her lace-making. Surely not Georgia's own mother?

Clark's voice broke through her musings. "Did you find out anything from Ravi at the funeral?"

"No, he did *not* want to talk to me. He's a very private person."

"Okay. I'll get Shona to give him a ring at work and tell him that you're coming in there. She'll make him co-operate."

ESTHER SPENT most of that day at school teaching the class one song. No one seemed to be listening and she couldn't really blame them. It was a gorgeous day and the blue sky beckoned.

She let them take their books outside for the afternoon. Sitting on a bench, she inhaled the spring scent. Someone passed around lollies and she took a raspberry one.

She watched Willow, who was moving around as if she had a scorpion in her trousers.

"Are you alright?"

Willow came closer and sat about a metre away. "I don't know." She sighed. "Do you ever think: Why me? I'm asking for a friend, of course."

Her intuition told her this wasn't a time to pry, just gently share a universal experience. "I have, and I'm not going to say that everything happens for a reason. But I think everyone feels like this now and then. All we can do is choose how we react."

Esther often wondered why it fell on her to make sure killers were brought to justice. It wasn't something she'd ever thought about doing before. But she kept that thought to herself.

After school, she walked across to the pharmacy. Shona's call must have done the trick as Ravi came out wearing a blue surgical mask and simply nodded. "Good morning."

He ushered Esther into a tiny room out the back, with a small kitchenette and shelves from floor to ceiling packed with boxes of medicines, impeccably labelled and stacked in alphabetical order. There were two large fridges with glass doors and surprisingly two tall desks with computer screens on top somehow fit in there too. "I'm sorry it's so small."

Esther waved away the apology. She didn't have to work in the tiny space, only visit for a while. She felt sorry for him being cramped in there.

"That's fine. I'm sorry for approaching you out of the blue yesterday. I know you are probably still having a rough time."

Ravi nodded and turned towards the computer, idly clicking the mouse on the lockscreen. "I am actually really busy too. But I'll answer your questions."

"Alright. Should we start with how you met Georgia?"

"I met her when we worked together over summer last year. So it was just under a year ago, I think. It was a horrible job and she quit after four weeks."

"Okay, where were you working? And how come she quit?"

"In answer to the second question, I don't actually know. She never did anything she didn't want to, from eating spicy food to taking the bus. The first question is simpler. We were working at a summer camp at Bewdley Manor. It was my last summer after finishing my degree. I wanted to do something different before my work got serious."

"What would you say your relationship was like?"

"Fine," he said, tightly.

"Ravi, you're still a suspect. We just want to find out what happened. For Georgia and so that it doesn't happen to anyone else."

"Alright, I suppose you would call it on-again off-again. We'd spend a few days together then she'd ghost me for a week. I didn't know what she was doing half the time. But right before all of this happened, she decided she was going to move in with me. It was going really well. Honestly."

"Don't take this the wrong way, but... Why have we heard from multiple people that you were quite possessive of her?"

He breathed in sharply. "Was that Georgia's dad? I bet it was. He wanted her to date other people. I was not so keen on that, which I think is understandable. At her birthday dinner in February, I was planning to propose to her, actually. Her father came out with all of that in front of everyone and I got really angry. Wouldn't you? He said she needed someone strong and confident, someone older. All this, while I'm sitting there with a ring burning a hole in my pocket. She stormed out, saying she didn't need either of us. I told the old man it was none of his business." He clenched his fists.

"Oh, Ravi. So you started work here? And she worked at the bar?"

"Yeah. She only did a few shifts each week. I think

she must have got money from her parents because she was never too worried about cash."

"Okay. And just take us through once again exactly where you were on the night of the first."

"Um, I was at the conference then in the bar. I went up to my room and went to bed about eleven. Call the hotel, they'll tell you."

"Do you know of anyone else she might have been spending time with? It seems like we have a lot of her time unaccounted for."

He shook his head. "I sometimes heard her on the phone. I don't know who it was, though. We both lived our own lives."

"Okay. And thank you for talking to me."

"My sister always says that I need to open up more. I sort of got into a pattern of not telling people about my life. It's why I became a pharmacist, actually."

Esther waited. It seemed like she was finally getting somewhere with him.

"I always cared about people. But if I ever tried to help them, they'd push me away. Even Georgia did that, I think."

"I'm sorry about that."

"Thanks," he said. "No one in my life wanted a man to be too sensitive. So I became a pharmacist in order to help people. We're the first point of call for the community. I've got a passion for herbal healing, too.

But my family thought I should go the traditional route."

That stopped Esther in her tracks. "I've got to ask this, but… would you have conium maculatum on the premises at all?"

His eyes widened. "No. Definitely not. It's a toxic plant."

She nodded.

"Oh." He gulped and the colour drained from his face as the words sunk in. "Oh."

CHAPTER 12

After another few days of no new clues, Esther decided to take matters into her own hands.

Mrs Haddock looked surprised to see Esther at her door, but quickly rearranged her face into a polite smile.

"I thought you might like someone to have a quiet tea or coffee with," Esther said. "I brought muffins." She held up a paper bag.

"Oh, yes. Fine."

"We don't have to talk at all. But I'm here if you want to."

They drank their tea and munched their baked goods in silence. When Harriet finally spoke, she said something unexpected.

"I've always wanted a cat."

Esther waited.

Harriet tucked her hair behind her ear. "Georgia wanted one too, but they were terrified of her. They'd hiss and carry on. She was heartbroken."

Outside, the wind had picked up and was shaking the trees.

"She was unpredictable. She would go to work sometimes and at other times, she'd be off who knows where. Of course, at her age, there wasn't much we could do. She didn't want to talk to us."

"Do you think she might have had another job? We can't work out how she supported herself."

Harriet sighed. "We're not sure. We've had our suspicions that she was dealing in something because of the mood swings, the disappearing for days at a time. But we could never prove it."

"It sounds like a very difficult situation," Esther said.

"Yes. He did kick her out once. Brian did."

"What happened then?"

"She got in contact after a couple of weeks. She said she was staying with a woman somewhere. We don't know who it was."

She lapsed into silence, fiddling with the tea cup, sitting it perfectly in the centre of the saucer.

"Harriet, do you know anything about the bracelet she wore?"

"That old thing? It was some sort of friendship bracelet, I think. She wore it all the time."

"Can I see it?"

"Of course," she said. "Follow me, if you like." She led the way up a narrow staircase and across the hall. The bedroom obviously belonged to Georgia, with a bright orange duvet and pillows in shades of purple. However, the rest of the room was sparse, with nothing on the walls and the dresser bare, except for a wooden jewellery box.

"Did you already clean out some of her things?"

"Hmm? No." She hummed a low tune to herself. "Oh dear, it doesn't appear to be here. Let me check in her coats." She held up a finger.

Esther looked out at the view from the bedroom over the park.

"No, I can't find it anywhere. Just like her phone, as well." She sat down on the bed and her eyes welled with tears. "I just keep thinking that if we had her things, we'd have a little piece of Georgia back."

"I completely understand."

Esther had an idea. "Hey, would you be able to teach me some lacemaking?"

"Oh! Yes, of course. I suppose it would take my mind off things for a spell."

They came down the stairs and into the little crafts room. Esther noted that the bunch of flowers was hanging in one corner to dry. She craned her neck to look as Harriet sat down.

"I've got the thread on the bobbins here. I'll stick a new pin in it here for you. Really, all I'm doing is crossing this one over this one." She picked up the second bobbin and placed it on the other side. "Then twisting these ones over these." She picked up the speed, flicking the bobbins over skilfully.

Then she stood up. "Here, you have a go. It's not hard if you start off slowly."

Esther followed the instructions. She tried to concentrate but she was sure that Harriet was hiding something.

"Would you be able to get me some water please?"

"Of course."

Harriet stood up and left the room and Esther immediately began pulling out the drawers. She spied a storage box that had a magazine picture poking out the top and pulled it out. She could hear footsteps coming down the hall. She fumbled to get the lid back on.

"Ah…"

Esther turned around. Emotions passed across Harriet's face - shock, annoyance, and then resignation.

"Are these what you took from Georgia's room? I knew it didn't seem, er, lived in."

Harriet nodded. "I'm sorry for lying to you. It's just that it has become such a habit. Georgia and I used to chat about the paranormal sometimes. Secretly, of course. She was very superstitious." She pulled out a poster titled 'Pirate Superstitions', which had phrases like, 'Never turn a loaf upside down once it's been cut' and 'Dolphins at night are a sign of good luck'.

"Why were you hiding all of this stuff?"

"My husband, Brian, is very particular. His family was hard up when he was a child and he has always had ideas about what we should buy and how we should behave. He says things like, 'money is what you do, not what you have'. He'd hit the roof if he knew I was encouraging her. He hated all the superstitious stuff because he thinks life is what you make of it. But I really think that Georgia thought she had something to fear."

"Alright. Is there anything else you've been keeping from us?"

Harriet looked up. "Fine." She took a deep breath. "Sometimes I buy it! You know, the lace that I sell in my online shop. Sometimes I buy it instead of making it. Lace-making just takes so long, you know?"

CHAPTER 13

"Alright, it's nearly time for the priest's mysterious meeting," Esther said. They were at their usual table at the pub, loyally patronising their local. It was a lot more empty than usual. "Feels like I've been waiting forever. You're still ok to come along on Friday, Aria?"

"Wouldn't miss it," Aria said. "It'll keep me from thinking about wedding photo locations. Church or community gardens, lake or gorge? It's exhausting."

Esther smiled in sympathy. "Great. Um, I'll get the next round, if you like," she offered. She secretly wanted to ask Jeremiah a few more questions.

"Same again, please," she said, when he looked up. "Do you mind if I ask you a couple of questions, too?"

"Now?" Jeremiah frowned. "I like you, Esther, but

you're nosy as anything," he said, polishing a glass without looking at it. "You have to give me something about yourself."

He'd caught her eavesdropping once before, so she guessed it must be difficult to trust her completely.

"Well, I'm a musical witch," she whispered, feeling an unexpected flush of pride. It wasn't something she had said out loud very much.

He leaned back, considering. "You're a musical witch? So your performance the other night at the talent show was some sort of enchantment?"

"No. Not at all. We just played our music. All above board. I have put a spell on people while performing before, though. By accident," she stated, pointing her finger for emphasis.

He dodged out of the way as if sparks would shoot out of it. "Alright. Impressive. I thought there was something supernatural about you." He spread his hands. "There is one thing I hadn't mentioned. So I've been an independent magic practitioner for a long time. It works for me to go it alone. But it's not for lack of trying by the coven. In fact, I was dating one of the women for a while. But it turned out that she was only using me to get me to join. They needed another hearth witch."

"Oh? Who was that?"

But he just waved his hand. "Their mindset is 'You're

either with us or you're against us' but I just want to do my own thing. I've always been a bit of a loner, I suppose. Bought this place at twenty-three instead of travelling like all my friends were doing. Anyway, Georgia had been talking to one of them and she wanted to join the coven but I was trying to persuade her not to."

"You think it would be a bad thing for her to join a coven?"

He nodded. "She does not play well with others."

"Right."

"Now, she's a bit different from me. I love my own company. I'm just as happy here when the bar is closed as I am when it's full of the regulars. She needs to have one or two people around her. But she'd be the one calling the shots, if you know what I mean."

Esther nodded. She wondered if Georgia was more like her father than either of them realised. "Your hearth magic, is that what helps you to return lost objects to their owners?"

He smiled. "I think so."

"One other thing. Her parents and her boyfriend both said she hardly ever seemed to be at work but she always seemed to have lots of money. They were both puzzled by that."

"Let me think." He brought out his phone and scrolled though for a moment. "She normally did two shifts a week. I guess I assumed she was studying as well. But I can't say I ever asked. She did always have nice clothes, though. New phones, nice shoes."

"Alright."

He set the drinks on the bar. "Whatever she was doing, I'll tell you that she could be ruthless. She did precisely what she wanted to and nothing more or less."

CHAPTER 14

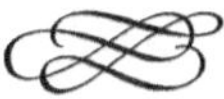

"Just call me if you need me. I can send Shona to you as quick as anything." Clark's voice was concerned.

"Aria and I will be fine," she answered. "Don't worry about us."

"Take phone. Call me."

What could go wrong? Esther wasn't afraid, since her anxiety had already made her run through every possible outcome of their little visit to their priest's house, but she was happy when Jay flew out the door to accompany them.

"What do you think will happen?" Aria asked, when they got into her Citroen. "And did you have to bring the bird in the car? What if it poops everywhere? I have to take my future mother in law out tomorrow. We're going to get her an outfit and she wants it to match the bridesmaids."

"Oh. Well, Jay won't do that." She turned around and fixed the bird with a stare. He cocked his head to the side, almost as if he was asking if that was a challenge.

"Ok, I'm sure no one would let us come here if it was dangerous, right?" Esther hooked her arm through her friend's.

"Unless this is a trap. Ooh, and plot twist: he did it!"

"Aria!" Esther knew her friend was joking but, somehow, in the late afternoon, it was harder to make herself believe it. The fog swirled around them, thick and damp. "It wasn't the priest. He didn't do it."

The knock sounded particularly hollow.

Pedro opened the door to them. "Young Esther," he said, kissing her on the cheek.

"This is my friend, Aria."

"You didn't bring the detective?" Pedro looked worried.

"No, I didn't."

Once they were seated in the lounge, he looked at her. "Thank you for coming, Esther. I must confess, I wasn't entirely up front with you. The person I was wanting to consult was my papa."

"Not the..." Esther pointed upwards.

The priest held his finger and thumb apart. "Well, a little bit. But my father was in the park as well that evening. I did get the kite down for young Mason but we were there before that. It's difficult to explain." He made a face and half turned away.

"I know it must have been horrible finding the body. Just let us know what you observed. It's alright. Take your time."

"That's not the reason for my hesitation. I've done many open-casket funerals before. No, what happened was this. My father heard things and he wanted me to go out there and have a look. This happened each month around the start of the month. I resisted for a long time, because I was afraid, I'm sorry to admit. I didn't want to see members of my flock, even from the past, wandering lonely. I'm there to guide souls, you see. I don't want to see some of them lost where I cannot help them."

"Guide souls?" she murmured.

Aria was nodding along.

"Ah, papa," he said, looking up with a smile when his father entered the room. "How are you today?"

The old man was in very good shape, wearing crisp black pants and a brown jersey with white collar showing. He had faded dark hair combed over to the side.

Pedro nodded as his father murmured something in Spanish. "This is the man, himself - my father, Bernardo Escarra. He has never learnt English. We've lived here for twenty years. He prefers to communicate in other ways," he explained.

"I'm not sure how long ago it was. He started hearing things at night when he was getting into bed. He started complaining about the creaking house. Then he said it was the trains. You did so, papa."

She waited while there was an exchange between them in Spanish. "He says to let him tell the story. Alright, fine. I will only translate it for you."

"Back when he was in Spain, after mama died and my sister had already left, he heard the neighbourhood dogs—no, he said the neighbourhood dogs all stopped. They were barking and whining and then, all of a sudden, he couldn't hear them. Silent as the grave. He went outside and stood in the garden in the bright sunlight and saw... my mother kneeling down there. Did you really?"

Another brief exchange with a lot of hand movements.

"Yes, she was totally focused on what she was doing. He didn't believe in ghosts but he knew grief well. He knew the shape of a loved one lost. He didn't say anything, just watched her. As he watched, he heard a specific high-pitched noise which got louder and louder."

Esther and Aria exchanged a look. "Like tinnitus?"

There was another brief exchange. "No, it was...

different. Nothing helped. He was almost driven mad by it, he says. For weeks and weeks, the noise haunted him. Nothing made it go away until one day when he spoke to her."

"What happened then?"

"He sat with her and spoke to her and when he stood up again, the noise came back."

"And this is what happens when he hears things in the park each month?"

"Yes, he hears the noises, getting louder and louder like the buzzing of bees, until he can't think of anything else so he goes out there and…"

"And what?"

"Keeps them company, he says."

"Who?"

"The spirits," Pedro said, with a shrug.

Aria let out a laugh but Pedro and Bernardo regarded her with calm stares.

"Each full moon, they come. That's why I arranged it for today."

"Ahem," Esther said. "Can you tell me, what do they do? These spirits?"

"This time they called to him. He knows they want him to help but he doesn't know how."

"So you can hear ghosts?" Aria asked. "Can you ask your father what he said to the spirit of your mother to make her leave?"

The priest laughed. "He says it's not fit for your ears."

"Did he do anything else that he can think of?"

"He whistled the exact notes that he heard. He's ashamed to say he got pretty frustrated."

Esther noticed the precise hand movements.

"Were you a conductor once?"

Bernardo nodded.

But it was Pedro who answered. "Many years ago."

"I'd love to talk to you about music. I've just taken a job as a teacher in a holiday programme class. It's chaotic, to say the least."

"I think conducting would be very similar. It's about working with the energy in the room. You have to make sure that you have the stamina to bring the musicians to the peak and be able to continue to the end. You have to make sure you lead. Like in any group, there are always some who need the soft approach and some who work better with a strict approach."

"Yes, I've noticed that, already."

"Oh, and they can spot someone who isn't confident straight away."

"That's useful."

"We wanted to introduce the idea of ghosts to you before you were thrown in the deep end. Are you both ready to see for yourselves?" Pedro asked, kindly. "I have to go and visit with one of my parishioners and papa has an ingrown toenail. That's why I was hoping Clark would be here, to go along with you. It's probably a bit old-fashioned but I'm extra cautious these days."

"Aria has three brothers," Esther said. "We'll be fine."

♫

"I'm not sure that we'll be fine," Aria said, when they were tramping through the park. "Where do you think we have to go? The park is pretty big."

"He seemed to think we'd have no trouble finding it."

"But he hasn't lived with you. You'd have trouble finding an apple at a picnic."

"Oh ha ha," Esther said.

The trees were still wet from the rain and every now and then, the steady dripping became a splash as water fell to the ground.

They got to the middle of the west field. It was difficult to see the lamplights along the path from here.

Aria gripped her tighter as it turned even colder. "I've got a bad feeling in my waters, as my mum used to say."

Dancing lights sprang up in the field; blues and greens, and a sound as if there were clamouring crowds of people. One of the lights resolved into a person, a person that was running very fast towards them.

Esther couldn't make out anything much apart from the hat bobbing around as the young man ran so he gripped it with his hand. He was very tall and ran in a clumsy way.

He didn't seem to be stopping. She let go of Aria's arm. If she didn't move, he would—

He ran through her. The last thing she saw was his chin next to her eye, then a chill as if she'd run through ice water. She turned, gasping. The man jerked as if he'd been hit and began to limp. He looked up and she noticed his strong nose and fluffy beard.

"Are you okay? Gosh, watch where you're going." Aria said to the young man. "You almost bumped into us."

"I think so," Esther answered. "Um, Aria. He appears to be—"

"I had to get away. I had to."

"Alright, you're safe. Er, what from?" she asked him gently.

"No, none of us are. They're making us go. Making us." He ran his hands down either side of his booted ankle, feeling around inside his sock.

"Go where?"

"I stepped in a hole. Look out!" he cried.

A man in a uniform came crashing through from behind them and stopped in front of the man on the ground. "There you are."

He dropped each word like a stone. Esther ran the other way and Aria was right behind her.

"You saw that too, right?" She asked Aria, who nodded.

"But shouldn't we try to help him?" Aria asked the question while walking quickly in the opposite direction.

"I fear it's way too late for that," Esther said. "Pun completely intended."

"You mean?" Aria jerked a thumb back the way they came. "That was them?"

"Yeah. We had no trouble finding them, at least."

A sloshing sound came from her right. They must be near the lake. She took a few steps forward, not wanting to see any more but unable to look away.

A woman, shimmering white in the moonlight, threw a stone into the lake from the bridge. She looked up at the sky. "I thought he'd be here by now," she said. "I thought he would have come." She looked down and trailed away.

A song made them look a little further. It was a jolly working tune like a sea shanty, and a ghostly woman was standing in the water, dipping clothes in and out of the river and rubbing them together. They watched for a few minutes but nothing else happened. Any singer was a friend of hers, Esther decided, and walked over, hopefully looking more confident than she felt.

"Hello."

The woman stopped her song and looked over at her. "Good evening, Missus."

"Do you know what's happening over there?"

"They're fighting," she said. "My older sister told me to carry on with my chores. You should be careful, though."

"And where's your sister? Is she involved in the fighting?"

"No," the young woman answered. She pointed.

"Okay, this is beyond silly," Aria said to her, as they walked through the trees. "Can you imagine Troy and Ashton having to explain to everyone that this is how we died?"

"They don't want to hurt us. I think they're wrapped up in their own problems."

They followed where the girl had pointed. Through the trees, next to the band rotunda, was a circle of people. Ghosts.

They looked like they were playing a game? Praying? Esther tiptoed closer. Aria was so close she could feel the warmth of her body.

Two middle-aged ladies were holding hands. The one they'd seen at the bridge stood just outside the circle.

"There's nothing for it. We need to do it now," one of them said.

"But we don't have the burdock!"

"Where is he?" called the woman with the baby in a plaintive wail.

"Wait for the moonlight to hit the cauldron and stir only once!"

They began a low chant. "By the moon, keep us safe…"

It was a coven of witches, she was sure. Esther looked down to see that Aria was gripping her hand tightly.

"It's alright, I think," she said. The presence of the witches calmed her, despite the circumstances.

They walked quickly to the edge of the park and back past the cottage that belonged to Pedro, only seeing one squirrel, that could have been translucent, or it could have been her imagination.

"Do you need me to stay at yours tonight?" Aria asked, when they got back to the car. "I'm happy to."

"I think I'm alright. I've got this guy protecting me." She stroked Jay's back.

Aria snorted.

"No, really. You should get yourself a familiar."

She looked back at the park, just in case. But the ghostly troupe had disappeared into the fog.

CHAPTER 15

$\mathcal{L}$ottie threw them a quick smile. "Just have a seat, girls. I've got a big order to take care of. We've got a charity breakfast coming in soon. About an hour."

They found their usual table by the window. This time, the plant pots out the window were green with lavender and colourful pansies showed their faces in between.

"Hey Lottie," she said, when their drinks arrived at the table. "So there's something I wanted to ask you about." She beckoned the older woman to come closer.

"Are you ready to join us?" Lottie smiled encouragingly.

Esther shook her head. Lottie was struggling more and more with the coven responsibilities and was always looking for 'new blood' to help with protecting the town. But, when Cara had asked her to join, Esther felt she could hardly look after herself, her kitten and her bird, let alone a whole town. And with witchy powers that were inconsistent at best and downright dangerous at their worst, she didn't feel she would be much help at all.

"No, I'm wondering if you know anything about a paranormal phenomenon here in Ledstow? Something that happens in the park every month with the full moon?"

"Oh, you mean the ghosts? Yeah, I've heard of it. Most of the locals have. Never looked into it too much, though."

"Of course you knew about it," Esther said.

"I sort of forgot about it, to be honest with you. It's one of those stories that comes up every now and then, usually when a group of teenagers dare each other to go down there on that night. The story goes that the spirits are protecting the town. They're harmless, anyway, and I've got so many other things to be getting on with around here." She narrowed her eyes. "How come?"

"Oh, we saw them," Aria said.

"Did you really? I'd like to hear—"

Just then, there was a rattling of crockery as a young man balancing a tray stacked with cups tripped just as he was heading into the kitchen. They braced for the crash but it never came. They all let out a breath.

"There's my new kitchen hand. I better go."

"Alright, Lottie. Thanks."

Aria took a deep drink of her coffee and let out a satisfied sigh. "It's hard to believe in anything like ghosts when you've got a strong, hot latte in your hand."

"Did I tell you about the funeral? Such a weird collection of people." Esther was thinking back to all the strange behaviour she had observed. "There were these shady-looking characters who came in halfway through. And Nell, the florist, seemed nervous or something."

"Ashton knows her, I think. He credits her with getting him his job."

"Really? There was also Hamish Falkirk, who set off my balderdash detector with every word. You know, the Tamagotchi guy?"

"You should find the dirt on him."

"I don't know how to contact him but I'll see if Clark can find anything out. And the last thing was that someone set off some sort of smoke bomb under the coffin."

"They're trying to scare you."

"Well, it worked!" Esther drained the last of her coffee and used her spoon to scoop out the marshmallow, which was deliciously melted. "You know, when I first got here, a tour guide told our group a story that ghosts walk the city walls protecting the town."

"I wonder if that was about our friends in the park? Or there could be more of them. Or the story might have changed over time."

"Yeah, the ruins of the old city walls are a couple of blocks over. I suppose if you imagine them as they would have been, it could have been a large rectangle."

"Those ghosts weren't protecting anything, though. They were doing laundry and running away."

"Yeah, it seemed like that first guy was trying to avoid fighting in a war."

Aria sighed. "It would be really helpful if we actually knew anything about history, wouldn't it?"

"Should we maybe do some research?"

"Good idea. I haven't got anything much to do today except decide on the wedding seating plan."

"I can help you with that, afterwards, if you like."

A crashing of crockery came from the kitchen and the young man stalked out the door.

"Are you alright, Lottie?" Esther called into the kitchen as they left.

She came to the door, looking harassed. "Yes, I'm fine, thanks. I just needed him to get out of the way so I could use a little cleaning spell. Know of any good staff?"

♫

"YOU LOOK for any mention of refusing to go to war in Ledstow," Esther said. "I'll look for any sign of groups of women or witchcraft from the same time."

"That'll work," Aria said.

They had already done a quick search online, but not having the dates or the names made things very difficult. Esther headed for the shelf holding books about the occult and spirituality. She carried a couple of large books over to a desk and sat down.

Cara, the librarian and another witch in the coven, gave her a quick wave. She was stacking shelves and seemed distracted.

Aria came over. She leafed through the book, stopping every now and then to read a paragraph closely.

A group of teens were chatting loudly at the next table and Esther had to raise her voice to be heard. "This only has generic information about witchcraft."

"I've found a book about conscientious objectors," Aria replied. "There were quite a few of them, it sounds like. They were court martialed, imprisoned and sometimes given hard labour. Listen to this: 'When I got to the camp, they asked me to put on the uniform. But I refused. They took away my own clothes and I sat there in my underclothes.'

"Oh my gosh. That must be what our young lad is."

"And this, from someone else: 'I had to go before a tribunal and plead my case for whether I had reasonable grounds to stay behind. I wonder if they think we are all cowards. But some of us simply want to save lives, instead of taking them.' It sounds like they objected for lots of different reasons; sometimes religious or moral."

She spotted the librarian coming past with a trail of kids in tow. "Cara, would you be able to help us?"

"What is it?"

"We'd like to know if there were any conscientious objectors here in Ledstow in World War One."

"Check out the digitised newspapers. Yeah, just a minute." This was to one of the kids. "There's an index as well. I'm slowly going through them, making sure they're all easily accessible. If there's anything about the topic, you'll find it in there."

"Perfect, thanks."

Aria sat down at one of the computers and clicked through to the past newspapers.

"There was a small group of conscientious objectors in Ledstow, who wrote letters to the paper. The military picked up most of them, except for a man called Peter Hopping, who died in the skirmish."

"Oh wow," Esther breathed. "Do you think we met Peter?"

♫

"PERHAPS WE'RE BARKING up the wrong tree with this ghost thing," Esther called out, later, when they were at her flat. "Ouch, Louis. Chill out. It's an expression," she said, as the kitten stretched out its claws into the juicy flesh of her thigh.

"No, I agree with you that it feels important," Aria said, coming into the lounge from the kitchen. "If only we knew somebody who was around Ledstow then. We could find out the full story." She placed two cups of tea on the table and wisps of smoke curled upwards from them.

"Mm. That would make that person 111 years old, if they were born at the start of the war, though." Esther took a tiny sip of the tea, which was scalding hot, as usual. Her tongue felt like it had been stung by a wasp. Aria must have a mouth made of steel. "I'm really interested in why they show up each month. That's not how ghosts are meant to work. I don't think they know they're dead."

"You might as well say that they are something we made up in our heads." Aria held up a finger. "But don't even think about saying that. You know that the priest saw them as well." She sat down on the armchair and Louis immediately stalked over to her and jumped onto her lap.

"True," Esther said, relieved.

"Let's hypothetically say that you were right," she started, stroking Louis' back. "How would we let them know that they are, in fact, deceased? How would we go about telling them something they had no reason to believe and don't want to know?"

Esther shrugged. "Oh, but we do know someone! Well, I sort of do."

The image of Iris "Zany" Grey, matriarch of the coven and ageless beauty from a long line of witches, popped into Esther's head. She'd lived here in town longer than anyone else she knew of. If Iris didn't know, then no one would.

♫

"WHAT'S THIS ABOUT?" Lottie asked. "Anything coven related can come through me."

"Oh no, it's actually about something that happened long ago."

"I see," she said, eyebrows lifting. "Well, it's a while til the next coven meeting, but I could meet you at Zany Grey's."

They arrived at the rest home. Iris was sitting in the corner, eyes closed. They quietly took a seat, listening to the comforting noises of the other residents down the hall.

"It's a long shot but we don't have any other way of finding the information. It would be wonderful if Iris could tell us anything."

"I'm sure she'll be happy to help."

"What about me?" The question came from Iris, who now had one eye open, just a crack.

"Sneaky old thing," Lottie said, but it was said with affection.

"Hmph. It's the best way to find out what's happening around here. Last week, I was the first to know that one of our nurses was pregnant."

"Alright, well, these young ladies have a few questions for you."

"I'm Esther and this is Aria."

"I know who you are."

"Oh, you do? Well, I know this is a bit strange but we are looking into something that happened here in Ledstow a long time ago. It involved the war and a young man called Peter Hopping."

"I don't know anything about that." She folded her hands in her lap.

"We think he died during the war but not overseas, right here in town. He was around six foot two, with a crew cut and really strong facial features, as well as a bushy beard. He refused to fight."

"Oh, bones be bound, I think I know of him. But only because my grandmother was best friends with his fiancée, Mary. Stay a while and chat with me. Then Lottie can take you to the coven archives."

"Oh, that would be great," Esther said.

"I saw you at the funeral," Iris said. "Georgia's funeral."

She nodded. "I was there. Are you part of the family?"

"No, I'm not. There were many there who weren't related to her." She pursed her lips. "But I cared for her a great deal. I was convincing her to join our coven as I thought it would be good for her to learn about magic craft with a group, to learn about moderation and sharing of power. I fear I set her on an even worse path, though."

Esther and Aria shared a look. "In what way?"

It was Lottie who answered. "We tried to have someone tail her but she was very good at losing them. A flash of steam, a burst of fire, they provided very good cover. We once heard that she had threatened someone. And now and then, we'd be asked to heal some pretty bad burns. But we still believed she could redeem herself. We still wanted to embrace her and her power."

"You keep all the coven documents in a storage unit?"

Esther looked at the identical garage doors on either side as they drove into the long driveway.

Iris had told them a little about Mary and Peter. Mary was waiting with the coven for Peter. But he never turned up. The witches had pressed on with their protection spell, but in the rush, they'd made mistakes. *They forgot the burdock,* Esther thought.

Mary had survived the fight and gone on to deliver a baby boy. Peter had never come home.

"Of course we keep them in storage. What did you expect?"

"I'm not sure," she said, sightly disappointed that there wasn't a secret cellar filled with candles, dusty books, and other mysterious treasures.

"We used to keep everything at Iris' place but, once she opened it up as a care home, we thought that it was safer in a locker."

"Probably."

Lottie parked the car and rummaged around in her purse for a moment. "Now, where is it, then? Ah." She got out and bent over to the lock. "I will ask you not to come in as there are protective charms that you might disturb."

"Ok, sure."

The garage door creaked up and Lottie disappeared into the darkness.

Esther stared out the window, thinking about the practicalities of modern-day witchcraft. A few puddles remained on the ground. The foggy morning had cleared and there were patches of blue amongst the clouds. One particular cloud caught her eye, making her shiver. There was that shape again. An oval with a hole through it.

"Esther, take this." Lottie dumped a huge book on her lap. "I've got a file of papers here."

Opening the cover, she flicked through a few pages. It was a scrapbook of letters, diagrams, and what looked like recipes. Treacle scones. Wartime pie. "This looks like the right time period. Alright, look here. It's a letter from a group of people who were against the conscription. They planned to defend themselves when they were called up."

Lottie looked over.

"Oh, look at this one. It's like the minutes of a meeting, maybe?"

"It looks like a coven meeting."

"'Peter raised the concern that magicals will be used as weapons if conscripted. As a bear shifter, he may be chained and forced to fight. Unanimous agreement. Voted to collectively defend the town from conscription using magical force.'"

A shiver ran down Esther's back. If that was the plan, something had gone very wrong. She held up another piece of paper. "This is strange. The envelope says it's from Peter himself. But it's blank."

Lottie took it and held it close to her face. She smiled. "Only to the untrained eye."

♫

THE KITCHEN of Lottie's café, Grounds for Divorce, was a calm place after hours. Esther folded her arms, watching Lottie strike a match and hold it to a long candle.

"Have you got the letter?"

When Esther passed the paper to her, Lottie held it near the flame. Letters slowly appeared.

Of course it was written in invisible ink. Sometimes, she seriously doubted her sleuthing abilities. Really, she should have been able to figure that one out.

Lottie read it out in a calm voice.

"'To my nearest and dearest, you know my thoughts on the upcoming fighting. Although I am not against the effort on the whole and I do not want to let down my nation, I have many complex feelings about this. You already know I am not a fighter. I'm a scholar.

My magical abilities mean I can heal twice as fast as others, so I will undoubtedly pass the medical exams.

With the latest conscription, they are calling up all single men who are fit and well. The officers are due to arrive in town tomorrow. If only your father had agreed to our marriage already. He cannot know that you're carrying a little bear. But I wish to stay here with you.

I won't show the officers my true form. If anything were to happen to me, know that I give my full blessing for you to find another who will love and support you.

Peter'

"I'm not crying. You're crying," Lottie said, putting the paper down to wipe her eyes with the heels of her palms.

"Poor Peter!"

CHAPTER 16

"Aren't investigations supposed to become clearer as you question more people?" Ash asked, rubbing his temples. "Not more confusing?" They were having a board game evening at her flat, but they'd gotten sidetracked talking about the investigation.

Esther laughed. "I think of it like a big pot. As you add more and more ingredients, the flavour becomes more complex. A little garlic, bay leaves, a sprig of rosemary, salt and pepper. At some point, it will have been simmering long enough that it'll be ready. It's a whole process." She waved her hand in dismissal.

"Or perhaps a cauldron?" Aria said, quirking an eyebrow. She was sitting on the couch, stroking Louis' back. The moment she arrived, the cat had turned from a prickly pine cone to a boneless furry rug, humming with contentment.

"Exactly. It does seem to work out in the end."

A movement caught Esther's eye and Jay flew in through the window that she had taken to leaving open for him. The bluejay swooped around the room a couple of times, making Ash duck his head, before it landed on top of the bookcase. Something dropped onto the game board and bounced onto the floor. It was a small roundish stone. As she picked it up, she noticed there was a hole all the way through.

"I think this is what my grandmother means about taking note of themes in my life." She told them about her dream, which had a similar shape symbol.

"What does it all mean?"

"I'm not sure."

Aria held up her phone. "Here, I'm searching it up. It looks like a hag stone. It's a stone that was thought to have magical properties, usually made of limestone or flint. Also called fairy stone, serpent egg, witch stone. Some even thought you could see fairies if you put the hole up to your eye."

"Cool." She put the stone into her pocket, feeling the reassuring weight of it drop in.

"Yeah. You can't go looking for the stones. They are meant to find their own way to you. Another legend states that the hole is only large enough to allow good fortune to pass through it. So it could be like a good luck charm. Then there's a lot of stuff about druids and snakes."

She looked up at the bird who was looking back at her, its head on the side. "Thanks for the present, Jay."

Esther's phone rang. It was Bernie Holland.

"Just a moment, guys," she said to her friends.

"Hello," Bernie said, in his posh voice. "I hope I'm not interrupting you?"

"Not at all."

"I'm so sorry I haven't been keeping in touch. It feels like days are just passing me by at the moment," he said.

"Oh, that's not a worry. I understand."

"The two week contract for the holidays is nearly up. But Esther, we are really happy with the progress you've made with the kids. How do you think it has gone?"

She took a deep breath. Was now the time to be honest or reassuring? "Good, I think."

"Great," he answered, almost without even noting her response. "There's a special concert coming up at school. It's a music gala. If you are agreeable, we'd like you to keep teaching them a few times a week up until the concert. It's only a handful of our students who will be performing but it would be nice to make sure they're at their peak as it's a fundraising concert. Can you please make contact with them as soon as possible?

Obviously, we'll keep paying you for your time. I'll send you the list and a rough idea of how many hours you should spend."

"Sure."

"Oh, that's much appreciated, Esther. Honestly."

She put the phone down and went back into the lounge.

"It's your turn," Ash said, indicating the game board.

"That was my boss. I've got a few more hours of work," she announced. "Helping some of the kids practise for a music concert. Sorry, but I've got to go and make some calls."

"Is that the end of the Pictionary for today then?"

"Yeah, I think it is, sorry."

She checked her emails and called Arthur, Willow, and Izzy, arranging to meet them on separate days.

Willow sounded worried.

"Are you alright? Is there anything you want help with?" Esther asked her.

Willow cleared her throat. "I'd like to practise with you tomorrow, if you can."

"Hey, it's normal to be nervous."

"You don't seem nervous," she argued.

"Well, I am."

"I feel like I'm going mad. I hear these noises. And my friend, she's always there. She never leaves me alone."

"That can be really difficult. You just need to communicate. Be honest. That's often enough. You can tell me more, tomorrow."

♫

THEY HAD ARRANGED to meet at Willow's home to practise, so Esther walked through Ledstow to the back, where the streets sloped gently upwards.

The house in front of her looked like a barn conversion. Large windows with no curtains gave her a view of the inside as she came up the path. Cream furniture and expansive wooden tables contrasted with the aged brick industrial facade of the building.

She knocked and a dog barked. Willow came to the door almost immediately with the culprit. She hauled the huge Dobermann back by its collar to let Esther inside.

"Hi. Um, just give him a moment. He'll calm down. Titan's friendly once he gets to know you."

Esther nodded. She wasn't about to push the relationship before the dog was ready, that was for sure. The dog's ears were flat and its body low as if he might like a snack of her fingers - and she needed those to play the ukulele.

"This way."

"What a lovely house," she said, admiring the antiques and heavily detailed furnishings.

The girl shrugged. "It's alright."

She followed Willow through into the main living area that she had seen from outside, where a grand piano shone from the corner. Willow told Titan firmly to stay and Esther sat on the opposite side of the piano on a dining chair that she pulled across the soft carpet. Willow pulled down her music book and started on the piece. She finished and Titan stood up.

"Alright, you can come over now, boy," she said.

Esther was still as the huge dog came over and sniffed the air around her, nose twitching. He stayed alert for a long moment, tail pointed straight out, then turned around and sat comfortably, leaning on her leg. Esther stroked down the dog's back.

"Just go through it one more time. Make sure to keep up the tempo in this section," she said to Willow, pointing at the bridge section of the music.

"Alright."

When she'd finished the song again, Esther turned to her. "You know, I think you're going to do just fine."

She shrugged. "Yeah, I know."

Esther lifted her eyebrows in surprise. "You do? Well, that's great."

"I really invited you over to show you something.

You are the only person who really seems to listen to me."

"Sometimes, it can seem like your family isn't listening. But they might have their own issues or not know how to help," she said, gently. She couldn't help but think of her own mother, who didn't seem to listen but often ended up helping. She meant well, anyway.

"Maybe we should just go upstairs to the kids' lounge. There's a TV up there."

"Where are your parents?" Esther asked as they climbed the stairs to the second storey which was nestled underneath the roof. Titan bounded up after them.

"They're out," she said. "Which is good because none of this would work if they were here."

"What do you mean 'work'?" Esther found a comfy-looking armchair and sunk gratefully into it. Willow was stretched out on the couch with Titan lounging all over her legs, his head draped over her knees. Willow seemed grateful to have her there. And Esther didn't really mind. The girl reminded her a little of herself when she was her age.

There was a buzzing noise and the lights flickered on and off.

Willow's eyes went wide. "She'll be grumpy because I've got someone round here," she whispered.

"Who?"

The dog lifted his head up and stared at the doorway. Then he whimpered a pitiful whine.

Willow pointed up at the ceiling.

"What's going on here, Willow?"

"I don't think we need to worry. She won't do much with you here."

"Who?"

Titan lifted his head as some noise came from downstairs.

"That might be mum and dad."

A small flame whooshed into existence in the air above them and went out again. Ghosts.

"So you've seen her before?" Esther whispered urgently.

"Not exactly."

"How do you know it's a 'she'? Have you communicated with her?"

"Sometimes, I think she wants something but then nothing will happen for a few days."

Esther bit her tongue. Ghosted by a ghost.

"Now, it's whenever I'm alone. Things move, flicker, spark."

"And you don't know who it is?"

The girl shook her head. A spark sizzled in the light switch.

"I might." Snippets of information that had been whirling around in her mind finally coalesced into an idea. A fire mage in life might have a shadow of her powers in death. The steam in the school corridor that she had mistaken for smoke. The steam coming from the coffin. The malfunctioning electricity.

"I don't know, but I think it could be Georgia Haddock. And I think she needs our help."

"Willow?" An adult called up the stairs.

The girl shrugged as she went to the door. "Yeah?"

"Come down here!"

Esther whispered, urgently. "She's local, the young woman who won the talent quest, you know?"

"Well, why is she haunting me? I don't know her."

Esther bit her lip. "Are you sure?"

She nodded.

Esther lapsed into thought. Perhaps some spirits got into a sort of holding pattern, their behaviours repetitive and unthinking. Like the group in the park or Bernardo's wife. These spirits could easily be shepherded to where they belonged.

Georgia was different. Her spirit was restless and sought vengeance. They had to find out who did it and stop them. Then it seemed, her ghost would be at peace.

SHE STOPPED in at Grounds for Divorce for a quick coffee. The rich smell made her look forward to the warming drink. Lottie was looking particularly harassed today, her cheeks flushed and hair coming out of its braids.

"Esther, you look like someone who can whip up a batch of muffins," she said, hopefully, when Esther came in.

"Do I?" At the moment, she hardly felt like she was in the land of the living herself. How could she go on with her life while Willow was being harassed by the ghost? The poor girl.

"Would you help us out with the cake stall? Jeremiah was going to help out but we can't expect him to now, of course. He'll be grieving, I expect. I know I'm pretty good but I'm not that good that I can bake everything myself."

"I'm sorry, I don't think—" Esther began, but Lottie cut her off.

"It's not for me. I'm just the messenger. But the proceeds go towards doing up the high school auditorium which is a very worthy cause. And the sale is during the music gala, so there will be heaps of people there."

Esther sighed. "I suppose I can."

"Great. Thank you, my dear. Baked goods need to be covered and labelled with the ingredients. Just pop them in here on Friday night and I'll take it all down in my van the next morning. I knew I could count on you."

Esther found a table, feeling like she'd just been hit by a truck. When the community rallied around in Ledstow, there was no getting out of it.

Just as she was about to take a sip of the coffee, her phone rang. It was Clark.

"Shona had a visit from the priest today."

"Father Pedro? What did he have to say?"

"He wanted to drop something in to the station. It seems he was walking through the park again and found something stuffed into a bush. Before you ask, I don't know why he was rummaging around in the bushes. Shona doesn't think it's relevant."

"What was it?"

"It was a florist's card that said, 'Meet me at the park at 10.'"

"Ooh. No name or anything? Who was the florist?"

"Petal to the Nettle was the name of it."

"Hmm. I'll go and see Nell."

There was a pause. "I don't know if that's a good idea."

"It's fine. I'll take Ash."

"Alright, then. I suppose that's ok. So if we think about what happened that night again, Georgia receives some flowers at some point. She thinks she is going to meet Ravi," Clark said. "Perhaps she thinks he came back early from his work trip and wants to surprise her?"

"It's still pretty odd to be meeting at the park at night. Especially when he hadn't been at the talent quest that evening. And also, if someone asked you to meet at the park, you wouldn't walk by yourself into the middle of the park where the lake is."

"True, you'd meet at the carpark. And this person had to know enough about their relationship to know that she would be keen to go and meet him. Remember they were on again, off again."

"Right, so that's a bit of a question mark. But then she drives to the park and realises it's not him. She doesn't scream or attack or anything. We know that because none of the neighbours heard any noise at that time."

"That's true. So whoever it was had to be someone she knew well."

"And trusted. Because she was really powerful and could look after herself."

"We need to find out who ordered the flowers."

CHAPTER 17

Esther did call Ashton but he was busy. She could wait for another day or she could just get it over and done with. Discretion may be the better part of valour, but time and murder investigations waited for no one.

Looking at a cute dog over the road, she walked into a large bunch of flowers at face height that were being carried by someone tall and slender.

"Ah, exactly the—" The tickle in her nose turned into a sneeze. "Choo! Sorry, I was trying to say you're exactly the person I wanted to see today."

The bouquet moved down to reveal Nell's face. "Me? How can I help you?"

"I was on my way to your shop to ask about a bunch

of flowers you've delivered. My name's Esther and I'm helping out with an investigation. I work just down there at the music shop sometimes." She pointed down the street.

"Alright, you better come into the shop with me. I've just been to the flower market and I'm about to open up. We start late on Mondays and Tuesdays." She paused. "And Wednesdays too, actually. In fact, most days I don't start until about nine."

"That must be nice."

"Ah, but I do work weekends. Birthdays, funerals and couple apologies don't stop because it is the week-end. Then there's the wedding preparations… They are an absolute pain but I get a lot of new customers from them. Ah, we're almost there."

Esther struggled to keep up with the woman, in both her walking pace and her speed of conversation, but she didn't mind. It was actually refreshing to chat to someone who spoke freely instead of in codes and secrets.

"You said you're investigating?"

"I'm sort of a consultant."

When they got to her shop, Nell went to put the key in the lock but the door swung open easily.

"That can't be good. What's going on?" Esther could already see that something was very wrong. She followed Nell inside the door where they paused for an instant. Nell picked her way to the side to turn on the light switch. When light flooded the room, Esther drew a breath. Flower bouquets were strewn on the floor. Some of the elegant tea cups were smashed. Pots and ornaments were on their sides.

"Oh, gods. My heart is breaking, Esther. I have worked so hard for this shop." The florist knelt down beside a large mirror, running her fingers over the edge of it. That was a strange thing to check first. She lifted it back up and gently hung it on its hook. She went over to the cash register and popped open the drawer, seeming relatively calm.

Esther peered around the shop, worried that someone was still in there. Her eyes flicked to the shadows in the corners. Then her eyes and nose started to tingle.

"Are you alright?" Nell said, when she saw her eyes watering.

"Oh yes, I'm just allergic."

She nodded once and her face was set, resolute. "Everything seems like it's still here. I'll go through all the stuff out the back."

"I've got to get to work right now," Esther said, grateful for the excuse. "But I'll check in on you later."

When Esther passed by the florist's shop again, she poked her head in to check on Nell. "It's just me," she called. Are you going alright?"

Nell looked up. "Thank you for asking that. I'm a bit shaken but I've got a lot to clean up. So I'm keeping myself busy."

"Come on, then. Let's go have a quick cup of tea next door. My nan always says 'If you look at things wrong-headed, they come out wrong' which I always thought was a weird saying. But now I've used it myself and it seemed to fit perfectly."

It was funny how those sayings made more sense as an adult. It was like using the right lens on an old microscope. Suddenly, the lens clicked into place and, with age or experience, you understood the weight of the words you'd heard so many times.

"Alright, then." Nell stood up and wiped her hands on her trousers, staring down at the mess, blankly.

"It will all still be here in half an hour," Esther said, gently.

"That doesn't actually help," she said, going out the door.

A little while later, they were safely installed at a table with cups of tea in bright crockery and a leafy, warming scent emitting from the liquid. "What about now? Feeling any better yet?"

Picking up the cup, she took a long sip. "Now, I believe you. Things really don't look as bad with a tea cup in your hand."

"They don't. So I just wanted to ask who sent the bouquet of flowers to Georgia Haddock and when? We think it might have something to do with her death."

"So you think it was suspicious? Ah, I remember that one, of course. It's a guy who comes in sometimes. Pale as anything, dark hair. Always pays in cash. He never signs who the flowers are from."

They lapsed into a comfortable silence. Nell was flicking absentmindedly through one of the free magazines on each table. Esther's mind was working overtime, thinking about who had broken into the florist's shop.

"Do you have any idea who might have done it?" Esther asked the question quietly, not really wanting to break the peaceful atmosphere.

She shook her head. "Should I?"

"Well, if you haven't found anything valuable missing, crimes like this are often done by someone with a grudge. Did you have any difficult customers recently... or perhaps unpaid bills?"

"The gods know I often have customers like that. Particularly in busy periods like around Valentine's Day and Christmas and especially when I have to raise my prices. I'm a single mother and every bit of what I earn goes towards uniforms, food and rent. And I get some jealous spouses, of course, who have seen a bank statement but didn't recall getting a bouquet themselves."

"Does that happen often?"

"Now, that I think about it, there have been two occasions in the past couple of weeks when I've had angry customers. The first was a young man who wanted to send a bouquet to his colleague at work. It seems to have given her the wrong idea, which his girlfriend is not happy about."

"And the second?"

"Well, she—" Her eyes opened wide and all the blood drained from her face. "But it wasn't!"

She drank the rest of her tea and walked out of the coffee shop. Esther scrambled up to follow her. But instead of going back into the shop, Nell walked up to a motorbike that was parked at the kerb, swung her leg over and undid the helmet that was attached. That must be why she always wore those thick pants reinforced at the knee.

"Where are you going? What about your shop?" Esther was a little worried about Nell riding off when she seemed to be in such a state of shock.

"What's going to happen? It's not like someone is going to break in."

"I see your point," Esther replied, but Nell was already revving up the engine to go. She rode down the street without looking back.

Esther waved out to Mark in the cheese shop, who had come out to see what the noise was, before going back inside.

The florist shop was gloomy in the fading evening. Trying not to sneeze as she walked past the rows of flowers to be cut, she flicked on all the lights. She looked for a broom out the back and began moving all of the pots and ornaments out of the area, so she could sweep up the spilled dirt. She swept it slowly into a pile and out the front door.

Sometimes, community was about rebuilding, raising funds, or finding murderers. Sometimes, it was just about cleaning out the bad energy.

AFTER A FITFUL SLEEP, Esther arranged a coffee with Aria. They tried to fit them in weekly, but they were both so busy right now. Aria was occupied with all the wedding stresses of the last month of planning. Esther was barely holding down three jobs.

"I should quit the music job, shouldn't I?"

"Not yet," Aria responded. "You can still decline shifts when your boss offers them. I think wait until you get something full time. You should cover for me while I'm away on honeymoon. I don't think they've sorted anyone out yet."

"I don't know the first thing about being front of house."

"I've got so many things to work out before we leave, anyway. Whoever said getting married was fun?"

Aria headed off for work but Esther had a couple of hours before the music practise. She took out her book to read.

It was quiet at the café today. One older couple were comfortably drinking tea in silence at the table next door. The place smelt of fresh baking and Esther settled into her muffin. Her phone vibrated on the table and she answered it in surprise.

"Hi Ash. You don't usually call me."

Her friend hated talking on the phone with a passion. If it was a choice between walking over nails or calling her, Ash was taking off his socks every time.

"No, but I thought you'd want to hear this." His voice sounded excited.

"Do I need to get a code-phrase or something to make sure it's really you? Where did we meet?"

"At my work."

"That could be anywhere. What did you say to me?"

"It was at the salon. I'm sorry, love, you won't suit

that cut. I'll get you a glass of wine and we can look at some better ones," he said, impatient.

She laughed. "That sounds right."

Ashton's words poured out like a waterfall. "Alright, I've had a chat to the producers that ran the contest today. They said that we can have the recording prize since we came in second!"

"You're joking!"

"Would I joke about this? That would be cruel."

"Oh my goddess! This is so exciting."

Once she had asked him at least twenty times whether he was sure, with his responses becoming more and more annoyed, he ended the call. Esther finished her muffin and coffee, excitement bubbling through her.

If they were going to be able to record, they needed a few more original songs. She pulled out her phone and looked at the lyrics she'd started a couple of weeks ago. It was a song about moving to a new place. She wrote a few lines, changed her mind and crossed them out, then wrote them again. When she looked up, she was all alone in the café. From the sound of whistling, Lottie was out the back.

She glanced over. Something had been left on the floor next to the table. It was a little notebook with a dark green cover. The front said, 'Working on a new me'. Esther made a face at the bland slogan. Inside were a list of names with dollar amounts. *Alright,* she thought. *What's all this, then?* She turned the page, looking over her shoulder to see if anyone was coming. 'Mark Handley $250.' That was the man who worked in the cheese shop. There was a note next to his name. 'Found cash on the ground and didn't hand it in.' 'Sue Spooner $700'. The names and phone numbers were written by the same careful hand in different colours of pen and it looked like a work that had been added to over many years.

What on earth? Esther flicked through to the end. 'Florist $100' and 'Knowingly made a poison and cannot lie.' The last two words were underlined several times.

Esther flung the notebook onto the floor and passed a shaking hand over her forehead. This was a list of things that each person in town had done wrong. Somehow, someone knew about all of them and had made a neat little list. She looked over her shoulder as she stood up.

Lottie was bent over looking for something in the fridge. "Lottie, can you do me a favour, please? Can you check if anyone comes back for that notebook and let me know who it is? Let's leave it there so they know where to find it." She had no doubt that someone needed that book and if they were from Ledstow, Lottie would know them. She also didn't want anyone to think that she or Lottie had read it. She had a feeling it was best to keep that quiet.

♫

NEXT, she met Clark at the pharmacy. Ravi's eyes widened when he saw who was waiting.

"Hello again," Clark said. "Can we have a word?"

"Sure. Just give me two minutes." He held up two long fingers.

They waited while he served the customers. Clark ducked under a hanging bunch of lavender, while Esther looked through the shelves of jars, labelled with everything from garlic to coltsfoot. She did a double-take at one of the jars and tucked the information away.

"Alright. So we just need to ask you a few more questions," Clark said, leaning against the desk.

"We found a card from a bunch of flowers inviting your girlfriend to meet in the park that night. She thought it was from you."

"I've told you I wasn't there. Can't you guys just leave me alone?"

"Oh, we know you didn't send it. But can you think of anyone who would want to frame you? We need to consider all angles."

He shook his head.

"Okay. Well, forgive the question but did you often

meet her in the park? We're trying to understand who the killer might have been and how they knew all about it."

He let out a huge sigh, shaking his head. "Alright. Yes, I did meet her at random places. We'd meet in the graveyard or the park and get some dinner or just chat. It wasn't for any suspicious reasons."

"So you were keeping the relationship hidden?"

"Again, it's not what you think. Neither of us were ashamed of it. I suppose it doesn't matter if I tell you now. But Georgia was involved in some serious business. She said it was for my own safety that she kept me hidden. She said that people might come after me. I think she was involved in something bad, maybe something illegal, alright?"

Clark and Esther exchanged a look.

"You told us earlier that she had agreed to move in with you? Did she think that the danger had passed?"

"Not that I'm aware of."

Esther folded her arms. "Why did you tell me that you don't stock things like hemlock? I saw something out there that was labelled 'hemlock'."

"Out there? It's not. We're leaning into the old world apothecary vibe in here. Most of those are just for looks. It's probably ground pepper."

"Okay. And you don't know any more about her business?"

"No. We didn't talk about that. I'm… not in trouble, am I?"

♫

THE IRRESISTIBLE SMELL of coffee wafted out as she went past Grounds for Divorce, pulling her in. She found herself in the doorway before she knew it.

"Needing a hot fix, are we?" Lottie looked up from where she was reading the newspaper behind the counter.

"What do you put in your coffee? I couldn't resist if I tried."

She tapped her nose with one finger. "Now that would be telling."

"A latte to take away, please."

Lottie nodded, folded her paper and stood up. "Have you got something planned to bake for this weekend? I'm sorry to keep nagging, but the organiser of the sale is really stressing me out."

"Yes, I was going to bake a couple of cakes."

"Perfect, thanks. Oh yeah, and someone came back for that notebook. I didn't recognise them, though."

"What did they look like?"

"It was a man of about thirty-five. He was pale, skinny and had dark hair. Just darted in, grabbed it, and went out. The sort of person you don't take much notice of."

"Thanks." Esther sighed. Who was this pale guy?

"What was it? The notebook?" Lottie asked, her voice casual, but her eyes were showing interest.

Esther guessed she must have had a peek inside. "I think it was a huge clue."

CHAPTER 18

$\mathcal{D}$espite the urgency, Willow's spirit friend remained silent for the next few days.

Esther was trying not to stress too much but the threat of something happening to Nell, the florist, was hanging over her. Would whoever it was come back to the shop?

She was so worried that she almost forgot what day it was until her phone rang, startling Louis off her knee, scampering off to find another warm spot.

She picked up the phone and saw it was her grandmother.

"Blue Eyes? Did you forget about me?"

Esther's eyes flicked to the calendar. "Never, nan."

"You did so. But I'll forgive you, of course, my love."

She sighed. "I've got a lot on my mind."

"You do, indeed. Do you want to put it off 'til another day? I've got nowhere to be."

Although the investigation was taking up most of her thoughts, an evening with her grandmother might be a nice distraction. "No way. I can be there in half an hour."

Esther took an Uber to pick up her grandmother. It was the night before her grandmother's birthday and a special night of celebration for them.

She stopped to pick up some supplies, before pulling up in front of the retirement home, where her grandmother was waiting with her friend Kevin.

"You look after her," he called, bending to wave through the window.

"I will, Kevin."

"Oh, stop your fussing," Hope said, but Esther thought she secretly looked pleased at the attention.

Esther lifted the suitcase into the back seat, while Hope made herself comfortable.

"I assume you've got the stuff."

"Of course."

"Good girl."

"How are you doing, anyway? I haven't seen you in a while. But you and Kevin seem very cosy."

"Oh, hush! And that's fine. You just come and see me when you can, you know that. I know you've got this new job as well as your blossoming relationship with the handsome professor."

"And a murder investigation. And a teenager who is being haunted."

"Ah yes. That's a lot for you to be worrying about."

Esther unlocked the door and pushed it open, then stood out of the way as her grandmother walked in, arm already extended. At the same time, Jay left his perch to land on her wrist. She brought him to her cheek.

"You must still have a familiar bond," she said, watching the interplay between the bird and the witch. She put her hands on her hips.

"I don't think so. I think it's just when two creatures are used to each other's habits, from a lifetime together."

"Well, I don't know if I'll ever get *that* used to him."

"He's not impressed about that," her grandmother said, as the bird gently nipped her ear. "And Jay is actually really helpful when he wants to be."

"I'll believe that when I see it," Esther said. "We don't need dinner, do we?" Esther asked, getting out her old handwritten recipe book and the ingredients. She quickly prepared the batter and put it into the oven.

Hope put her hand up for Jay to fly off. "No, we don't." She poured them a generous glass of red wine each. "Do you remember the first time we did this?"

"Of course. I was staying at your old house the night before your birthday party. I got up because I was hungry in the night, with the smell of baking wafting everywhere. I thought I'd just find an apple or something but the cake on the bench was too irresistible! I grabbed a handful from the side and stuffed it in."

"You must have only been five or six." Her grandmother laughed.

"I heard you coming and thought you were going to tell me off so I hid in the laundry. But instead, you sat down and called, "Well? Are you going to join me?""

"So you crept out and sat down. We played cards for hours, if I recall right."

"And ate the whole cake. It was magical."

"Well, really, why not? Life is fleeting as anything, so eat the damn cake."

"Agreed," Esther said.

"You know we won't always be able to do this, though," her grandmother replied, after a pause. "I am getting older, despite all my efforts to the contrary."

"But we can now and that's what matters."

When the oven timer went off, Esther pulled the cake out of the oven, stuck a knife in it to check if it was cooked, and turned it onto a plate.

"That smells divine," Hope said, as Esther placed the cake onto the middle of the table and the heavenly scent wafted between them. It was a caramel brown colour with orange strands of carrot visible through-out. "Look, it will be alright. I know it."

As they ate slices of the tender cake, warm and un-iced, Esther felt that she was right.

♫

IT WAS ONLY MUCH LATER in the evening that Hope revealed why she was so optimistic.

"I have an idea."

"More cake?"

"Well, yes," she replied, comfortably. "And we could make contact with the spirit, ourselves."

"What? No. Absolutely not. I mean, how? I thought you were never taught anything about being a witch?"

"Yes, that's true. When it comes to our specific sort of music magic or 'harmonies', as I prefer to call it, I had to find out everything for myself. But it doesn't mean that I didn't pick things up along the way from other witches."

Harmonies. Esther liked that. "You're a medium, now?"

"No, I don't call myself anything like that. But I have dabbled now and then with mixed results."

That was how Esther found herself hunting through the storage cupboards, looking for magical items.

"We don't need a whole altar. I'll be happy with a few candles," her grandmother called out.

"Will this do?" Esther asked, coming back and dumping the fruits of her search on the table. There was a yellow beeswax candle Esther had made when she was a kid, a tall blue candle in a sun and moon holder and a tea light candle in a low glass cube.

"Should be fine. What's her name, love?"

Esther wrote it down on a notepad. The noise, when she ripped the paper off to pass it across to her grandmother, was loud in the quiet night.

Hope closed her eyes and began slow breathing. "I find it's getting easier to cross as I get older."

For some reason, that alone made a shiver run up Esther's spine.

Her grandmother hummed a note and held it. After a few minutes, she spoke again in a low, monotone voice.

"Georgia Haddock. Georgia Haddock. Georgia Haddock. You leave that young girl alone and come talk to us. Speak to us."

A squawk rent the air and Esther's heart hammered in her chest.

"Silly bird!" she said, rather more angrily than she meant to.

Her grandmother grinned. "He gets funny with the supernatural. I think he's sensing it through the bond."

"Uh huh." Esther closed the door.

"Let's try again, eh?" Hope said, her voice cheery. "Georgia—"

I'm here, alright? Jeez.

The voice was lower than she'd expected, and sort of husky. They both froze, looking at each other in the flickering candlelight.

What do you four want?

"Four?" Hope asked.

You two, the cat and the bird that are listening at the door. I can sense all souls.

Hope pointed at Esther, who spoke up. "We... we're trying to work out who..."

Killed me? Why? I don't even know you.

"Well... "

You think I'm nice because I acted nice at the pub? At work?

"Georgia Haddock," her grandmother said in her best impression of a mother who was rapidly losing patience with a naughty child. "We are trying to help you."

Well, this is funny. Some witches trying to help me. A bitter laugh echoed thinly around the room. *I don't know who did it. Does it even matter?*

"Yes, it does, Georgia," Esther said.

I just felt very unwell. I thought I was going to meet someone—

"Ravi."

But they weren't there. I was overheating, so I lay down in the lake.

"And you didn't see any sign of a person? Not a shoe or a piece of clothing? Anything?"

Not a thing. But I've got my suspicions.

"And what had you eaten or drank before that?"

It was the chocolate, of course. It came with the flowers. Haven't you done any research at all?

"Chocolate, right." Hope wrote the word 'chocolate' down on the piece of paper.

Look, if you really want to help, speak to Ralph Houndtooth. At the launderette.

"We will help you, Georgia. But you have to leave Willow alone."

CHAPTER 19

"You did a séance last night?" Clark's voice sharpened immediately. She imagined he was staring into the distance, probably already imagining the research he could design and wonderful theses he could write.

"Yes. With my grandmother."

"Why do you always do these things when I'm not there? I would have loved to observe something like that."

"I know, I'm sorry. But that's just how it worked out. I couldn't have stopped my nan, even if I'd wanted to. She's very... determined."

"So that's where you get it from?"

"Maybe, maybe. When are you coming back, then? End of the week?"

"Hopefully. I can't wait to kiss you."

"You can kiss me soon enough," she teased. "But seriously, should I go to this laundrette?"

"Esther," he said, in a cautioning tone. "You should absolutely not. It would be a ridiculous idea. It could be a trap."

"It's a laundrette. How bad can it be? And why would a ghost send me into a trap?"

"Georgia was pretty ruthless." He was quiet for a moment, then said, in a long-suffering voice, "At least take someone with you. Please."

♫

THE LAUNDERETTE WAS a small but brightly lit shop on the main street. Esther had hardly even noticed it before, squashed as it was between the corner shop and the antiques store. It didn't look too forbidding.

She smiled at the old man behind the counter. "We'd like to speak to Mr Ralph Houndtooth."

"He's in the back." The man jerked his thumb towards a door.

They opened the door and ducked under hanging bed covers and duvets. That distinctive drycleaning smell pervaded everything. There was another door in the back.

"You think it's this one?" Aria asked.

Esther shrugged. "Hello," she called into what looked like an empty office.

"Why hello there," a tiny creature said, as he jumped out from behind a cupboard door.

"We are looking for Mr…"

"Houndtooth. That's me. Come in, come in," he said. He went to the door, looked out and pulled it to behind them. It clicked firmly shut.

"Nice to meet you…" He put out his hand to shake and left a pregnant pause for them to say their names.

Esther reached down and shook it but kept her mouth shut.

The figure was about a foot tall, but of a solid build. He was wearing a black suit. He had long dark, brown hair in a mullet and a grizzled face with a patchy beard.

Ralph sauntered over to a small armchair, sat down slowly and clasped his hands. "Meet my boys," he said.

A side door that Esther hadn't noticed swung open and three tall hooded figures trooped in. They had to be at least six foot three and they stood in a line by the wall. They looked suspiciously like the ones that had appeared at the funeral. This was quickly going from a fun encounter with creatures of folklore to 'danger, Will Robinson'.

Mr Houndtooth lifted his chin. "These young witches have come straight in like they own the place. They didn't know the proper shake. And they wouldn't tell me their names. Rude, very rude. What do we do with people who don't give us their credentials?"

One of them smirked.

"I'm sorry for my friend," Aria put in quickly. We were sent here by Georgia. Georgia Haddock."

Ralph narrowed his eyes.

"She was a good friend," Aria lied, smoothly. "She mentioned your name and that you were trustworthy. Oh yeah, big fan of yours. And now that she's…"

"Gone to mix with the tree roots," he offered.

"We wondered if there's anything you could tell us that might help us figure out what happened to her." Aria's arm slid around Esther's back, in silent support.

"You mortals are always obsessing over what kills you. You just have short lives, alright?"

"So can you help us?"

"Liars."

"I'm sorry?"

"I know you were lying. Nobody's a big fan of mine." He held up a hand. "But there are certain individuals for whom I hold a grudging respect. And Georgia was one of those. So, for her sake, I'll help you. Sit down."

They sat.

"Real talk, now. When I heard that something had happened to her, I had my suspicions straight away. But we can't exactly turn them in ourselves. I got one of my guys to steal a piece of evidence that would lead to the killer and leave it in a popular place in town." He raised his eyebrows as if that should mean something.

Esther was at a loss. She looked around the room. One of the guys was particularly washed-out and his cheekbones stuck out. A wisp of dark hair poked out of his hood. "The notebook?" Her voice came out in a squeak.

He nodded. "I may not always believe in the justice system. But I believe in justice for my friends. I suspect it was Georgia's partner who killed her."

♫

DESPITE THEIR QUESTIONS, Ralph wouldn't tell them anything more direct than that, as he said he wasn't a snitch.

"I thought he wanted us to find the killer," Aria grumbled, after they left the laundrette.

"We're lucky to leave there in one piece," Esther said, letting out a nervous giggle. "But I have to say I've almost gotten used to everyone speaking in codes and half-truths. No one wants to implicate themselves in anything so they all talk as if it's someone's birthday coming up. I put the 'you know what' in the 'you know where'. It's exhausting, honestly."

"It is. What did you think he meant about Georgia's partner?"

"Well, I don't think he meant Ravi. I think Georgia was working with someone else. Ralph mentioned that his guys placed the notebook in the café for someone to find and that that should be enough to find the killer."

"What if it was the florist and she staged the break-in to divert attention? You said the notebook mentioned her?"

"Why would she call herself 'the florist' though? I wish I got a better look at the stupid thing."

Ralph had said they had returned the notebook to its owner so that whoever it was wasn't suspicious. Esther was interested in his strange sense of ethics.

Ashton was just walking around the corner to her flat when she arrived. "Oh, good timing."

"How's it going, Ash?"

"I'm good. Do you want to get some dinner?"

"Let's order in," Esther said. "I'm exhausted." She unlocked the door.

"Good idea," Aria agreed.

Ash looked at her with concern. "You need to look after yourself. I think you're doing too much."

"I'm definitely doing too much. But if I can just get somewhere with the case…"

Her friends came in and sat down. "Souvlakis?"

"Ooh, yes."

"I'll order from the place on the corner," Aria said.

"Hey, do you know who I saw yesterday?" Ash looked up at her, eyebrows raised.

"No, I couldn't possibly guess."

"Ham Falkirk. He saw me down the street and just started chatting about his new venture. He's opening up a B&B that's advertised as haunted. It's some farmhouse on the edge of town. He's going to be doing haunted tours, too. I think he thinks we're friends."

"Sounds like he's here to stay?"

"Yeah, it does."

"Maybe he thinks, because you're both musicians, that you'll have something in common."

"He got a call from his mum while we were chatting and he had to go. She was always really bossy. But I didn't tell you the best part, he wanted me to advertise the B&B at the salon."

"Wow. Some people."

"Right?" Ash got himself a beer from the fridge.

They passed a pleasant evening, eating soft pita bread filled with tasty lamb, chatting of this and that, and laughing at in-jokes. Murder investigations didn't cross Esther's mind once.

CHAPTER 20

CLARK

Clark removed his glasses and rubbed at his eyes. He hadn't told Esther that he was coming back early and he toyed with ringing her and pretending he was still in Edinburgh. She'd love it when he turned up a few hours later. She'd pretend that she didn't but her face would light up and her cheeks would go pink. He loved making her feel special.

He couldn't help but think about her asking about what the next steps were. He had his doubts, although he knew what he wanted. He'd acted like it was fine but the fact that Esther's mother had spelled him unsettled him. It wasn't just himself that he had to think of. It was

Triss, too. Magic undoubtedly had a dangerous side, as they were seeing with Georgia's case. He shook off the thoughts.

Esther was only part of the reason why he was excited to go back. He had an EMF tool in his bag to test where they did the séance. He would also ask Esther to introduce him to Willow and check out the electromagnetic readings at the house. After all, it was important to check these things out rigorously.

Although he was open-minded about the paranormal, his past experience had taught him never to take things at face value. One example was the placebo effect of parapsychology: If people have a strong belief in the presence of paranormal phenomena, they may perceive random circumstances as evidence of psychic ability. As a result, biased reporting or overestimation of the impacts may occur. He always had to account for the most logical explanations.

"Sorry," he said, as a reflex, when a large man kicked his bag that was poking out into the aisle. He pulled it back next to his feet and held onto it.

The man sat down in the back of the carriage and stared out the window, his shoulders slumped forward.

There couldn't be anything that caused doubt to be cast on his research. That was why their experiments were often conducted without either the participants or the researchers knowing what the specific test was - or double blind experiments.

A prickly feeling on the back of the neck told him someone was watching him. He turned his head casually but the man wasn't looking at him anymore, if he had been.

Clark shrugged his shoulders. The trees and fences passed by in a blur out the window.

They pulled into the station and people began to stand up. As he lifted his bag, it seemed lighter. He opened it up and checked inside. The EMF meter was missing. Alright, this was fine. It wasn't worth hundreds of dollars at all. He bent down under the chair and checked underneath. A man humphed as he edged past him to leave the train.

If he could get some evidence of the spirit, it might get his supervisor off his back for a while.

He spotted it. There - under that seat. He reached for it, breathing a deep sigh of relief, and put it in his bag. The carriage had emptied out. Now, the competitive edge spurred him on. He rushed to leave the train and stepped through to exit. How strange that the EMF reader had fallen out. It wasn't exactly small.

Blinding pain slammed into his head and he put his hands out to break his fall.

HE KEPT FALLING. The noise was gone. There was no longer any sense of weight, no limitations of the body— only a boundless, tranquil light surrounding him.

Nothing hard or cold. Nothing painful. No time. The sensation is otherworldly, as though he's floating in a vast, infinite space.

There's no ground beneath his feet. The light that envelops him is warm, comforting—a brilliant, glowing presence that feels alive with energy. It is soft but intense, as if it pulses with the rhythm of a heartbeat.

He feels an overwhelming sense of peace, as if every worry, every burden, has dissolved. The weight of skepticism, from the years of scientific inquiry, from the emotional walls he's carefully built around himself, melts away. There is no fear here—only peace.

The light narrows slowly to a circle. As he moves forward, he sees a figure ahead. It's a glowing, indistinct shape. The figure is standing in front of a vast expanse of... stars? Or is it an endless ocean? He can't be sure, but it feels like a threshold between two worlds. The figure seems to beckon and he feels drawn to it, understanding that it holds a key to something he's been seeking his entire life.

He moves forwards, the movement like a dream, forever chasing.

But just as he reaches the figure, the light moves

further away. It becomes smaller and smaller. He is a star in the infinite sky and he is burning up.

♫

No, not burning. Pain, that was the word. Splitting headache. Perhaps it was a good thing that he could feel something again. Life is pain. That means he's alive. He opened an eye and saw two faces above him. It was not his time.

"Oh mate, we thought you were a goner." One of them said, his face white and dancing around like a flower in the wind.

I was, he tried to say, but it came out as a croak. Why couldn't he speak?

"We've called an ambulance. It will be here soon."

"Stay awake, please."

His eyes closed.

♫

"Aiden Thomas. Aiden Thomas. Hello?"

Someone bossy was calling to him. Female. Was it Esther? No, she didn't call him that. Only Triss did when she was trying to annoy him. His mother used to, too. He spoke without opening his eyes. "It's Clark," he tried to say.

"... Aiden? You've had a concussion."

A concussion? It all came rushing back to him. The train. Being watched. The hit to the back of the head.

He opened one eye. A young doctor was staring at him, her glasses perched absurdly on the end of her nose. "You're safe. You're in the hospital."

The void. The figure. The tunnel. The comfort and peace. This world felt harsh and bright in comparison.

He thought of Esther and a warm feeling spread through him. She was the best thing in his life.

He forced his fingers to move and grabbed onto crisp linen sheets. "... time."

"Pardon? You might get some pain and dizziness for the next few days. That's completely normal."

"It wasn't my time," he croaked.

CHAPTER 21

"You were attacked! Oh my gosh, are you alright?"

Clark had waited until they were both sitting on the couch to tell Esther what had happened. It was lucky he did, as she looked as if she might faint. Her eyes were wide in a face devoid of colour. She patted his arm.

"I'm absolutely fine," he reassured her, with a smile. "It still hurts a little, though. But they said I was very lucky."

"I'll say."

"You don't know the best part, though."

"What?"

"I had a near death experience!" He leaned forward, eager to describe it to her.

"Only you would think that was the best part of getting hit over the head." She shook her head in disgust. At least, some of the colour was coming back to her face now.

"This is not the sort of surprise I envisioned when I decided to come back early. But it was a real and true N.D.E. I've read a lot of the research about them. This included the strong light, the tunnel, the feeling of peace, all of that. I was moving towards the other side." He paused, as words didn't seem to be able to do justice to what he experienced.

"That's terrifying."

"No, it wasn't at all. Reassuring, really. I knew that it wasn't my time yet. But some day, it will be."

"Can we change the subject maybe? This makes me so uncomfortable to think about. Would you like some toffee pudding? With ice cream?"

He nodded enthusiastically, then touched his hand to the back of his head. "Maybe I'll keep the nods to a minimum."

She stood up to get the dessert, looking over at him as if to make sure he was alright.

She came back holding two bowls and passed one to him. "I think you should step down from the case." She held up a hand. "No, listen. For one, you are obviously needed back at the university and B, I think you might be in danger. This attack has to be related to the case.

People here in town know that you're working on this. Someone must have followed you."

Clark didn't think she'd appreciate him pointing out that she'd used 'one' and then 'B' for her list, so he closed his eyes for a second. He took a few breaths. Was she right about this?

"I've put in a police report about the incident, for what it's worth," he said. "Shona is doing the paperwork for the incident too. I don't envy her that."

"And? How is that going to help if someone wants to finish what they started?"

"There's something else. Something changed in me the other day. I'm no longer afraid of dying."

She gave him a look, her head on the side. It was a look that you'd give a strange insect that appeared in your garden, one that you'd previously only read about. Curiosity, but also disbelief.

"If you're still in this, I am too."

"Are you sure?"

"I'm sure. I have my doubts about the reason that I was called back, though. It all seems very convenient, in light of what happened."

Esther put her hand to her mouth. "Someone wanted you out of the way."

CHAPTER 22

"Alright, let's go through the group song."

Willow shrugged. "I can't find my music book."

"Really, Willow?" Esther tried to hide her exasperation but one day out from the concert, this was just careless. "Arthur might be able to lend you his."

"I think it's *her.* She doesn't want me to play music." She rolled her eyes to indicate the ghost.

"Well, why would that be?"

"I don't know." Willow tied her hair back off her face.

"She's after something." Esther kicked herself as

she realized that the stone wasn't a present at all. Jay was giving her a clue. She pointed to the bracelet. "That."

Willow took off the bracelet. "This old thing? It's hardly going to be worth anything."

"Not for you. It was almost an amulet for the person it belonged to." Esther ran it through her fingers. It was all very obvious, if you thought about it. Mismatched blue beads and a grey-white stone with a hole through it. "Hag stones or witch stones have a long and fascinating history. They are imbued with power and are very special to witches. They are thought to be protective."

"That must be what she wants," Willow breathed. "I swear I didn't know."

"Of course you didn't." Esther smiled at the girl. "Can you tell me exactly where you got it?"

"I tend to pick things up. I've always noticed things other people don't, like little treasures. People call me a dreamer."

"I know what that's like. When people think you're a dreamer, I mean."

"They aren't even necessarily worth anything. I think I found this when I was with my friend and we went to her mum's work."

"Who's the friend?"

"Angeline. Her mum's called Nell."

"I DON'T THINK it's strong enough," Clark said, when she relayed the information to him.

"Nell sent the bouquet to the victim. And the victim's bracelet was found there. There's too many coincidences. Surely, that's enough to arrest her."

"I need evidence, though. How am I supposed to back that up? Do a séance at work for Shona?"

"No, get Mrs Haddock to identify Georgia's bracelet. She'll do that. And Willow can make a state-ment about where she found it. I've let her keep it for now, but she knows it's important."

"Alright, I'll give you that. But why was the shop burgled, then?"

"Maybe she did it herself? She did discover it when she was with me, which is awfully convenient."

"She didn't know she was going to be seeing you, though. You said you bumped into her."

Esther slumped. "Oh yeah, that's right."

"Look, I'll do it and we can question her but I think it's all too simple."

"NELL?" Clark asked, inside the interview room.

Esther watched from behind the glass.

"My name's Nelgreen. That's my true name. It's unusual, isn't it?" She drummed her fingers on the table, staring off into the distance. "You can trust me. I've given you my name."

"Yeah, it is unusual. Do you have something you want to tell us?" Clark waited, his facade of patience belied by the twitching of the muscle in his jaw.

"I was only trying to bring a little joy to people."

"What does that mean?"

"I came here for a new life. My bouquets make people better friends. They enhance platonic love and trust. How is that a bad thing?"

Clark frowned.

Esther tapped herself on the forehead. Of course - the notebook had said that Nell couldn't lie. She texted Clark: 'Ask her straight out if she made the poison'.

"Where were you on the night in question?"

"I was at work. I had a big order to go through for the next day."

"What was it? And can anyone verify that?" He looked down at his phone, adjusting his glasses. "Er, did you make the poison that killed Georgia Haddock?"

"Was it hemlock?"

Clark looked up at her. She guessed they had their answer.

"It was."

"Then I think I might have made it." Nell looked

down at the table, then she looked up at Clark. "But I promise you I didn't know it was poison."

"You made a poison but you didn't know it was poison?" He stood up. He was getting even more frustrated and his voice dripped with sarcasm. "Do you expect me to believe that?"

She spread her hands. "The person who requested it was asking me what I used to use back home. I listed out some of the common herbs we infused into gifts. And when I said hemlock, they asked if I could make some. I... said I could, because at home, hemlock is like coffee. For our people, it brings extra energy."

"What do you mean, your people?"

"I'm from beyond."

Clark shook his head and came out the door. "Did you hear all of that? Absolute rubbish."

Esther shook her head. It was all true and everything she had been wondering about Nell until now made sense. "Can I?" she asked.

"Fine."

She opened the door and slipped in.

Nell looked up in surprise. "Oh, hello. You and him are...?"

"Partners," she confirmed. "I know he's pretty grumpy, but this investigation has been a really long and twisty one, with lots of dead ends." She snorted at her own pun.

"I'm telling the truth," she said.

"I know."

Nell visibly relaxed. "Oh, I'm glad. So you understand I'm one of the fae people? I can't lie ever. I can put plant magic into anything but I try to use it for good mostly."

"I thought it must have been something like that. Who was it who asked if you could make hemlock?"

"It was that same pale guy. I chat to him about motorbikes, sometimes."

Esther put her head on the side. It really felt they were circling closer to the answers. But they all pointed to an underworld of crime going on right here in Ledstow.

She shook her head. There was no time to dwell on that now. She had to go home and bake several cakes for the cake stall.

As they had thought, Nell's alibi checked out. Even Clark seemed downhearted as he reported it to her.

"Look, we've got a takeaways delivery driver that popped in just after nine. Nell forgot to eat til then. We have her daughter and Willow who walked down there about nine thirty and mucked about in the shop until she closed up at eleven."

"I knew she was telling the truth. But now we're stuck with who ordered those flowers?"

"Wasn't it the guy from the laundrette?"

"Yeah, but who ordered him to order them? We know that Ralph's group worked with Georgia and her partner. So someone told him to send the flowers."

"Someone who was trying to blame Ravi and take attention away from themselves."

Esther lapsed into silence. Georgia had become extremely superstitious. She'd obviously suspected someone was after her. Even as a powerful mage, she'd thought that her rituals would save her.

Perhaps they would have, Esther mused. But perhaps the murderer took the witch stone bracelet off her after she was poisoned.

CHAPTER 23

The school hall was about three-quarters-full, stuffy with the fug of breath and body odour of teenagers. Willow was nowhere to be seen.

There was a table off to the left for the cake stall. It was empty and baking was piled on the ground beside it. As Esther watched, Mrs Falkirk came in, shook her head, and straightened the table cloth. She sent her son Hamish off to fetch something with a flick of her wrist.

With another click of her fingers, she commandeered a nearby young person to help her set out the food. Next, she pulled a pile of cardboard tags out and got another child to fold them and write on them.

"I made this. It's a zucchini cake made with vegetables from my garden. Put five pounds on it."

She really seemed like somebody who got things done. That was fine, you needed people like that.

"You, dear," she said, casting around and fixing on Esther. "Can you run to the kitchen and grab the rubber gloves and serviettes? We have to remember our hygiene standards. Can you believe they didn't set it up?"

"Um, sure. Through this way?" She waved towards a door in the back wall.

"Yes."

She went through into the little kitchen and grabbed the bags of supplies. A door in the other end led out into the corridor. A familiar voice floated to her and she hurried down the corridor. Was Willow with someone else?

"Willow? Are you ready—"

The girl was huddled in the corner, her hair streaming down her shoulders, music book hugged to her chest. Books were flying across the aisle, dipping in the middle, and slamming onto the shelf. One fluttered open and a few pages fell out and fluttered down to the ground. A magazine flew out and slapped into the wall.

Esther hid back around the corner and called out to the girl. "Are you alright?"

"No, not really," she called back.

"No, I suppose not. Can you come out?"

Esther peeked through the bookshelf. The girl shook her head.

She ran through, books missing her by inches. One glanced off her head. Esther grabbed onto her and held her tight.

"I can't take this anymore," she said. "It's almost every time I'm alone now."

"I know. It's ridiculous," she raised her voice. "Ridiculous. Leave her alone."

"You can't just order her round."

"I know. But I've got a plan." She didn't have a plan, so much as a vague idea. But the girl didn't need to know that. She needed something to put her faith in.

Alright, think Esther. It would be a lot easier to think if books weren't flapping and snapping at her head. "The ghost is shy so she won't show herself in the hall. You go and do your performance. Do you think you can? I'll cover you," she said.

"Take this." The girl thrust her hooded sweatshirt at Esther and ran through to the hall, pausing for only a second at the door to look back. A book hit into the glass a second after the door swung shut.

Esther leaned back against the trophy cupboard to find some relief but it seemed the books were giving up, finally. Smack.

SHE RAN around the corner and almost slammed into Clark.

"Is Willow playing?"

"I don't know," he said. "She's probably finished by now. But wait. Are you alright?"

Esther paused. She must look a mess as she'd been hit by at least five books. She nodded once, then raced up the stairs to the wings and looked out at the stage, where Willow was standing up, to a large round of applause.

Phew, she was alright.

Willow sat down and pulled out her music book. She started the first piece. This was the one she was most confident about.

Esther walked around the back of the hall and passed the gloves and serviettes across to Mrs Falkirk, who took them gratefully. "How is the sale going so far?" she asked.

"Oh, pretty good. We've got some beautiful cakes."

"I made that one," Esther said.

"Lovely. And I made this one." Mrs Falkirk's cake was in the centre and it was three layers tall, a magnificent green buttercream creation.

"Wow."

"Yes. Everything made from scratch."

Esther's eye settled on something that decorated the

bottom layer. They were little brown frogs. "Did you, by any chance, make those chocolates?"

"Oh yes, I did," she said.

There were price tags written in a familiar hand, too, with the same distinctive seven as the notebook.

Esther's smile froze on her face. But there was no time to think because a loud pop came from the stage. Willow.

Esther ran up the steps to the edge of the stage, dodging kids who were waiting in the wrong place. She stepped out into the lights.

"What's she doing up there?" she heard someone call. It was Mrs Falkirk.

"Maybe she's going to sing."

"At a children's concert?"

"Always sticking her nose in."

Esther ignored the noise. Willow had her back to her. She was getting ready for the second song and placed her fingers on the keys. She began to play the starting chords, then moved onto the thirds.

When she got to the arpeggio part, a high-pitched noise started up. Willow froze and looked at her.

"And rest for two beats," Esther called. "And start again."

Chords. Thirds. Arpeggio.

A clunking came from the piano and it began to

shake. Willow glanced uncertainly over at her, eyes wide.

The ghostly visits flew through her mind like a classical piece of music. There was the intro when Georgia had appeared in the school hallway, setting the scene with wisps of steam. There was the verse at Willow's house where she learned more about what was happening. Then there was the chorus; the ghosts in the park returning each month. Then the bridge where Georgia threw books in the library and now, this was the high point. This was where it all came together. This must be the time to finish it.

Esther lifted her baton, and began to conduct. She listened for the exact pitch of the ghost.

The notes shortened as if the piano strings were being tightened. A string snapped. She cast a glance at the piano. So much for that beautiful instrument. It was done for.

With one hand, Esther beckoned to Willow to keep going.

In the chaos, Esther's heart beat fast. Willow looked at her, the whites of her eyes visible all around. How could she reassure the girl when she had no idea what to do herself? A shard could fall on her or Willow. A piece of debris could hit her and knock her out again. She'd be blamed for what was happening.

She listened. Behind the pinging of strings, the

cracking and banging of wood, she heard something. It almost sounded like a high-pitched tone. Was this it? Did she have to somehow send the ghost away?

But if she used her magic, it could go wrong. She could let out too much and hurt Willow. She could damage the hall. A black key flew past her ear with a whizzing sound. She felt the flutter of anxiety threatening to break through. A trickle of sweat ran down between her breasts.

But if she did nothing, it wouldn't stop. In fact, Georgia might bring her fire magic next. Willow trusted her, Esther, to help. So she would have to trust herself.

Esther whirled her magic around in a large circle, visualising the ghost and began to sing the same tone. Two hammers flew from the piano and landed on the floor.

The ghost stepped out and stood with her hands on her hips, a scowl twisting her face. Obviously, they had angered her enough that she'd lost her shyness. She reached for Willow, who reared back.

The ghost of Georgia shook her head and reached for Willow again. Her half-transparent hand passed towards the girl's neck and tightened. Esther took a step towards them. Could she make it in time?

But the ghost's hand retreated from Willow. Something was dangling from her fist. The bracelet.

She was having trouble holding it with her unearthly hands. She reached out with both hands and held onto it, pulling it to her chest.

This was it. Esther tightened the circle, as if she was lassooing a large beast. She sung the finishing tone, which came to her, as if from nowhere.

Georgia's face cleared and her head tipped back. She reached out as if to muss Willow's hair, in a strange, affectionate way.

Esther held on, her magic, muscles and voice all strained.

The ghost faded away.

CHAPTER 24

CLARK

He followed Esther back into the hall. "Hey, wait." She had disappeared again. He shook his head. She'd almost looked like she had been in a fight.

Clark sat down to wait next to a man on one side and an elderly lady on the other. He supposed Esther would need to be close by for the kids she taught.

The man was not even pretending to watch the concert and took out his phone. Clark leaned back slightly further to see what he was looking at. It was a terrible habit he had got into since working in the police force. Before that he'd never been this nosy. You see, it wasn't enough to think someone had done some-thing. Evidence was vital. It worked well with his science background.

Intuition went a long way, though. Even the way this guy sat was suspicious, his shoulders hunched and leg shaking.

The man went into his Instagram and checked out a couple of photos of himself in a music band. Clark turned around again. Where was she? He spotted her over by the cake stall and stood up. As he did, he noticed the man's thumb paused as he scrolled. He hovered over a photo of a blonde lady. She was behind a bar. It was Georgia.

He strode over towards the cake stall but now he couldn't see Esther. There was a queue of people waiting to purchase baked goods. She popped up and now she was running towards the steps. What was she doing? He stopped in the front of the stage, looking on in shock as Esther crept on at the back. She was confident while performing, but this was stretching it too far. Was she going to play a surprise duet?

The girl paused at the start of a song, then resumed playing. There was a popping and a cracking sound. It almost sounded like the piano was breaking to pieces. He had to hand it to Esther, that was a pretty cool effect. It really elevated this one from most kids concerts.

Esther darted forwards and the whole piano rocked. How on earth had they done that?

Now Esther was posing in the middle of the stage. No, she was struggling. He jumped up to get to her and dizziness overcame him as he was on the edge of the stage. His head swam. Oops, it must be left over from the concussion.

He very nearly fell right off but grabbed on to the edge of the stage and managed to make it to Esther, who was holding onto Willow's hand. "Get away," he thought he heard her say.

"I'm here."

She seemed to shake herself off and come to. "Clark?"

Everyone clapped, then stood up and cheered. The hall thundered.

Esther blinked a few times, then grabbed his hand and they all bowed.

"Are you alright?"

"Yeah." She bundled Willow off the stage and found her parents. Clark followed her.

She and Clark looked at each other. "Alright," they both said at the same time.

"You go," she said.

"I saw that guy over there, looking at photos of Georgia," he said, pointing to the second row.

She followed his finger. "That's Hamish Falkirk," she

responded. "Well, I found out that his mother makes her own chocolates." She let the phrase drop, expecting a response.

"And?"

"The poison was in the chocolate that was delivered along with the flowers."

"Oh! So one of them gets the poison from the florist, adds it to the chocolate and… gives it back to the florist to deliver to Georgia's house?"

"Thereby framing Nell neatly for the murder."

"Right. But which one?"

They both thoughtfully started packing up chairs when the concert ended. Clark was lost in his thoughts. He kept looking back at the man with the beard, sure that he was the same one who was staring at him on the train.

It was decision time. He could wait to arrest the guy and question him in the station. He looked over at Esther, who seemed distracted, too. Knowing her, she was probably going to talk to him herself. He'd better get in first so that she didn't put herself in danger.

He waited for the guy to leave the main hall, then headed after him.

"Hamish Falkirk," he said, standing tall as he could. "Where were you on the night of the first of April?" He flashed his badge, which he kept in his pocket. "I know you attacked me and dang near killed me on the train."

The man's eyes darted to the side but there was nowhere to go except for the bathrooms. "April first. I was here in town getting ready for the music contest."

"And after the contest?"

"Had a drink after. Then I went to my friend's house. He can vouch for that."

"What about in between?"

Hamish had his back to the wall now. "Alright, I also went to the park."

That caught Clark's attention. "The park? Why?"

"It's stupid," he said.

"This is a murder investigation."

The man balked. "I was encouraging the priest to go outside and see the…" The end of his sentence trailed off.

"What?" His voice came out as a bark.

"Ghosts." Hamish ran his hand through his hair. "He'd been getting up in church saying that people shouldn't believe in them. I thought I'd show him that he was wrong. It was my mum's idea."

"Why on earth?"

The man huffed. "Because my new business is haunted accommodation. I can't have people thinking that it's all rubbish. They have to believe that Ledstow is an old ghost village."

"You're under arrest," he said. "Stay there." He pulled out his phone to call Shona.

ESTHER

It was as they were packing up that Esther snuck off, only feeling slightly guilty. Clark had told her to wait while he went to the bathroom. He'd said Shona and Derek would turn up soon enough and they could take Mrs Falkirk to the station for questioning.

Esther watched him go, guiltily. She was going to put herself in the spider's lair. She figured that Mrs Falkirk was small-framed and wouldn't be able to overpower her. The woman hadn't shown any violent tendencies so far, except for the poisoning, which wouldn't be a very good weapon face-to-face. Clark would no doubt say she was being ridiculously foolish. But she needed some answers.

Mrs Falkirk was cleaning the dishes from the cake stall. "Ah! Look at all of these. You'll help me, won't you?" She threw a tea towel at Esther and she caught it by reflex.

"I'm here to talk to you."

"You are? Is it about the bake sale? It went very well."

Esther's pulse raced. "No. It's about Georgia Anne Haddock."

The words dropped into the kitchen like stones into a pond.

"Who?" The woman's demeanour changed in an instant. Her eyes locked onto Esther's.

"You know who."

"How on earth did you link me to her?"

"It wasn't easy. But I had help from some people who wanted to see justice for Georgia," she said.

"She wasn't as nice as you think. Very powerful and almost drunk with it. That's why she was so useful."

"You used her for your little extortion racket."

"We had a nice little gig going. She'd made noises about stopping but I never thought she would. Then she wanted to be completely honest with Ravi. But the whole thing would fall apart without her. It wouldn't work. So I made a plan for some time in the next year. I was going to pin it all on him."

"Then I had to bring it all forward, didn't I? I saw her practising a week before the show and knew she was going to win. She would have ruined everything. She actually told me that she'd written a song exposing everything. How silly is that!"

"We know you got Nell to make up the hemlock. How did you get the poison into the chocolates and then back to Nell to send? Without her realising?"

"I simply made up some plain chocolates and delivered them to her shop as a sample pack on the same day. The courier driver is easily bribed. I did the switcheroo with the poisoned chocolate and I asked him to deliver the flowers just after she got home from the talent quest."

Esther thought that was a risky plan. Someone else could have easily eaten the chocolate.

"One thing I can't figure out is how you and Georgia met."

Mrs Falkirk smiled. "It was years ago when she was working at the summer camp. I visited as I was teaching the kids how to make sweets. Hamish saw her first and took an instant fancy to her, but she wasn't interested in him, unfortunately. She started working little cash jobs for me as she hated it there; ringing up people who owed money and all that. Then when she discovered her fire magic, she couldn't wait to show it off. But I am always keeping score and so I knew that she'd stolen money from her father. Once you have something over a person, you own them."

"That's awful." Esther felt sick.

"No, that's business. No one else ever knew that we knew each other. Her phone would be the only evidence of our communication. And I took that and the little charm bracelet."

"But she didn't want to be your weapon anymore, did she? She was moving in with Ravi and she was going to get married. She didn't want to be used."

"Don't be silly. You never really get out of this world. Because it's a lot easier than the way people like you do things. If you've ever been really poor, you'll know there's no way you'd want to go back to that."

Esther's heart beat faster as Mrs Falkirk came closer. She took a step back.

"So you killed her?"

"Well, yes. No one's impossible to get rid of. If only we hadn't been so ridiculously nosy, eh? If only we hadn't got all caught up in someone else's business," she said, her voice dangerously soft.

Esther spoke quickly to distract her. "Who attacked Clark? Was it your son?"

"Who's Clark?"

"The policeman. On the train." Esther moved to the side a little, trying to make some distance.

"Ah."

Up close, what Esther had thought were kind eyes seemed cold as ice. If Mrs Falkirk was a lion, she would have spotted a weakness in her prey. They faced each other for a second, each calculating their next move. Mrs Falkirk gradually moved her hand to the right, groping for the large kitchen knife that was on the bench.

"Get away from her!" Clark roared as he burst into the room, face red. His hand slammed down to stop her wrist. "You do not have to say anything. But, it may harm your defence if you do not mention when questioned something which you later rely on in court. Anything you do say may be given in evidence."

"I don't know what all this fuss is about," Mrs Falkirk said.

But Esther could tell she was uncertain now. She reached into her pocket and pulled out her phone where a recording symbol was clearly visible.

"This says otherwise."

EPILOGUE

"You know, I've been wanting to ask you something," Clark said. They were sitting on the couch together in her flat. Jay was sitting on the arm of the couch. Louis was staring at them from the floor, looking upset about the indignity of it.

"What's that?"

He took off his glasses, which he always did when it was something serious.

"I want to ask if you'd like to move in with me."

"Oh." Esther was taken aback. He'd never mentioned that he was thinking about this. "To your place? With you and Triss?"

"I know it's a really big move. You can think about

it. But we do spend a lot of time together so from a practical standpoint, it makes sense."

"I honestly haven't considered it," she said. "And I've got my bird and my cat as well. They can be a lot to deal with." The bird was standing on the edge of the couch and fluffed out his feathers. "Sorry, Jay."

Clark waved away her protestations. "When I had that near death experience, it was almost like coming back to this world wasn't the right thing to do. Like the *other place* was somehow better. But I knew that it wasn't time for me yet and thinking of you anchored me here. I want to cook you breakfast and sleep in late with you on the weekends. I want to check in with you each day about what we're having for dinner." He put his arm around her. "I'll admit that I had been a little worried about how it would go with Triss but after seeing how you've been with Willow, I have every confidence in you."

"She needed me," she said, simply. Esther saw a lot of herself in Willow and was trying to be the person she'd needed, as a teen. She had explained that it was the ghost that was breaking the piano and Willow's family had helped pay for a replacement instrument for the school.

He took a breath and met her eyes. "You're already home for me. I can't imagine waking up without you beside me, or coming home and not having you here.

And I want more of those moments. I'm not asking for forever right now, just a chance to see what it would be like."

Esther bit her lip. She leaned forward and kissed him firmly on the mouth. After a while, they broke apart. "I will… think hard about it," she said. It was a very big step to move in together with a child involved. Would that make her a step-mother? Or step-sister?

"What about all the magic stuff?"

"Triss can deal with it. She'll love it, actually."

Esther put her head on the side. "And you?" She remembered his comments about how it was difficult to believe in magic when it was happening to him. Was he still in denial?

"It's real. All of it," he said. "Magic, the afterlife, everything." He mumbled something.

"What was that?"

"You were right."

She laughed. "Anyway, who did attack you in the end?"

"Really funny story," he said, drily. "Simon Whalley, the new guy, arranged for the university to call me back there so that he could have a good look around."

"What?!"

"Shona hit the roof when she found out and sent him packing. But I'm sure they'll send someone else across eventually."

"Then Ham Falkirk came in, looking for me, and Simon told him exactly when I was coming back, which train and everything."

"Ah, that has to be a breach of protocol."

"I guess Simon thought the rules were more relaxed in a small town? I don't know. He'll get a slap on the wrist."

"Well, I suppose everything's come out in the wash, now," she said, echoing her grandmother. "Mrs Falkirk will go to jail. But she did not want to implicate her darling boy."

"No, she even sent him to the priest's house to get him out of the way when the crime happened. But he told us everything. There is one other thing though, why did you tell me to go away? On the stage? I was just trying to help."

"I didn't," she said, surprised.

"What do you mean?"

"I'm pretty sure I didn't say anything to you."

"Maybe it was Willow, then. I heard it."

"When exactly did this happen?"

"Well, I climbed onto the stage. You were poised with your hand in the air."

"That was when I was conducting the ghost into the afterlife."

"I accidentally touched the blue bracelet that you were fighting over."

"The ghost's bracelet?"

"Oh my god." He groped for a piece of paper and wrote down a few words, his academic side shining through. "I didn't want to believe it."

"What?"

"I think I've developed psychometry. You might call it second sight. Basically, it's communing with the energies attached to an object. I heard the ghost say those words. Not just that, I could feel her disgust." He was frozen in place, whether in excitement or shock she didn't know.

She put a hand on his arm. "Maybe your near death experience made you more sensitive."

"Yeah, maybe."

She breathed out. "You can communicate with the dead. That sounds pretty magical to me."

THE END

A NOTE FROM K M JACKWAYS

HELLO! Many thanks to my wonderful beta readers and those lovely people who read everything I write. Thanks always to my husband for encouraging me through the difficult times, finding those sneaky New Zealand-isms, and picking up the slack at home.

Thank you also to my parents, who have always been there.

I HOPE you enjoyed Treble Death. In this book, I wanted to explore our relationship with ghosts, and with life and death itself. A fourth book in this series is coming soon featuring Esther and Clark investigating a murder at a wedding. In the meantime, why not read about the adventures of Cara, the Ledstow librarian, in the fae realm, in A Twist of Faerie?

A TWIST OF FAERIE EXCERPT

At Halloween, when the dead leaves are taken into the ground and the veil is thin, it is said that a whisper can echo through worlds.

CHAPTER 1

"Trick or treat!" The kids' voices screeched.

"Here, have the rest of the bowl." Cara felt sorry for the children, who were just on the edge of growing up and looked a bit awkward. Some had made a half-hearted effort to dress up as pirates. She waited until they'd taken handfuls of wrapped lollies, then shut the door lightly.

"That's my good deed for the year," she said, catching her sister's eye. "And a blessed Samhain to them. Now we can ignore any more knocks. Unless it's that hot fireman I've been waiting for. I'd definitely get the door, then."

Serena smiled. "You're a witch," she said. "You should be able to make it happen."

Serena was four years younger than Cara, but

looked nowhere near her 29 years, with her clear skin, large eyes above ruddy cheeks and long fingers resting lightly on the bench, as if she could float off the earth at any point. Serena's long, fine, blonde hair contrasted with Cara's own heavy brown bangs that never sat right. They couldn't look more different.

"It doesn't work like that," Cara reminded her. "Witchcraft is subtle and you have to tease it gently, not force it to your will. I'm not looking, anyway. No one will ever live up to the male characters in books."

But three wines later, she found herself mixing up a potion. She threw in sage, rosemary and, of course, mustard seed.

"It was once called eye of newt, you know," she said, over her shoulder.

"I do know. That smells good," her sister said, reaching her hand toward the cauldron.

"Careful." Cara said it automatically. Looking out for her sister was as much a habit as scratching her nose. 'Take your sister along,' her parents used to say. 'It will make her happy'. So she took Serena with her to her drama class, to her friends' houses after school, to her first job at the supermarket.

Serena was a crying, colicky baby. As soon as she touched the cot mattress, she cried. She wouldn't lie down. She couldn't sleep. She was too small, too pale. She wouldn't grow, wouldn't feed. She scratched at her head with tiny fingers and left red, raw lines. Cara saw her mum grow drawn and stressed, and her dad became snappy and gradually spent more hours at work.

Then when Cara came into her powers in her teens, she was able to see what was wrong with her sister. She learnt about potions, adding herbs to her sister's meals for fatigue and trouble sleeping, and ground up plant powders for concentration. She gave her potions for reflux. She experimented with salves and ointments to help her itchy skin. It helped a little, but there were new symptoms each week.

Serena had been to so many doctors and they always told her that she should get better in a few months. Her life had always been a delicate balance between being social and preserving her energy.

"Oh well, at least we lasted longer than last year's Halloween party," Serena said, pulling a blanket around her shoulders.

"Lottie understands. And witchcraft is the perfect end to the day. Come on then, write your wish on this piece of paper." She pushed the notepad page and pen towards her sister.

Serena raised her eyebrows at the engraved fountain pen. "Does it have to be a fancy pen?"

"No, witchcraft doesn't depend on that. But I have

to use them some time. What should I save them up for? Letters from my death bed?"

Serena shrugged. They often used gallows humour to deal with the fact of Serena's illness and her sister was a master of the dry retort. "Might be nice."

"Alright. Quick bit of housework." Lifting her palms up and curling them slowly into fists, feeling the power build in her forearms and wrists, Cara sent it out towards the dirty dishes, which wiggled and jumped into the dish rack, perfectly clean.

Serena laughed. "Goddess, that one never gets old," she said with delight. "If only I could do that. It's so unfair that I get the chronic illness and you get the witchcraft!"

"Well, that's why I'm here for you." Cara said, lightly. "Now, let's get on with it."

"You are," Serena replied, tilting her head to one side. "What shall I ask for, then?" Her sister held up her wineglass and swished it around. The liquid caught the light, as if whole worlds were caught inside the glass. Ruby worlds with crimson trees.

Cara knew what her sister would write. For the last few years, Serena had been desperate for a family of her own. At one point, she had a partner. Matt. They had moved in together, and were happy for a while, but they eventually broke up. Serena arrived at Cara's tiny flat in Ledstow village, pale and drawn, and moved into the little room upstairs. Her sister would wish for a family.

"Perhaps someone will be listening one day," Cara mused, out loud.

What about her own wish? Cara visualised a strong, sexy fireman who treated her like a princess. One who stayed to share breakfast and understood the love language of funny memes. Wouldn't that be lovely?

She sighed one of those full-body sighs, put her own pen to the paper, and finally wrote the same wish as ever. It was what she had been whispering every first star of the evening and each time she blew out the candles on her birthday since she was young: 'I wish for my sister to live a long, healthy life.'

"What are you huffing about?"

"Oh, nothing. Tonight feels like a good time for a re-watch of Practical Magic."

Cara dropped the pieces of paper into the cauldron, where they disappeared with a flash of light and a sizzle, and reached for her glass of wine.

THE NEXT MORNING, Cara woke up late. She wrapped herself in her dressing gown and wandered out to the kitchen. Serena was nowhere to be seen, but there was a piece of note paper on the bench. 'Gone to get bread x' was written across the page in Serena's light, curved hand. The kitchen smelt of cleaning liquid and there was no trace of last night's drinking and witchcraft.

Her phone alarm buzzed at her and Cara looked down at the screen. The planting! Lottie had made her promise she would turn up to the tree re-planting as a representative of the coven. It started ten minutes ago.

After the quickest shower known to womankind, Cara threw her clothes on. Pulling her coat around her, she grabbed her phone, before stepping into her gumboots and sloshing across the wet leaves. The horse chestnut tree outside brought shades of gold and bronze to the grey, damp day.

She stopped at the corner supermarket before ascending the windy road. "Have you seen my skin and blister today?" she asked Nigel, the old man at the counter who knew everyone in town.

He reached under the counter for his 'Closed' sign and stretched to place it at the end of the conveyor belt.

"Ah, yeah, as a matter of fact," he said. "Serena was talking to that lad who just started here for work experience. Think he was stocking the shelves. Tall, skinny fellow who really thought the world of himself. Haven't seen him again this morning, either."

"Right," Cara had said, slowly. Her protective instincts were already stabbing at her spine, but she made herself relax. Serena was an adult. She'd lived by herself.

When she arrived at the planting, the others were about to drop their saplings into the holes dug for the trees. The local newspaper photographer was standing nearby, with his camera on a tripod.

The town lay below a clinging fog this morning; Ledstow, her first love, a town whose bricks were spread with the mortar of love and protection. She could see the church steeple and the top of the oak trees around the cemetery peeking from the cloud. Cara waited until the photo session was finished, drawing her coat in the autumn chill.

People came to Ledstow for a new life. Some of them passed through the library, and she helped them with whatever they needed. She didn't ask a lot of questions. They turned up in town because they needed a haven. They had nowhere else to go or nowhere else they wanted to be. But the cloak of protection only extended so far, and there were those who resented the magicals and non-magicals living in harmony. It was up to her and the other witches in the coven to protect the town's peaceful state. Mostly, that meant keeping up the protection charms and keeping tabs on any suspicious activity. But the coven worked together with other community groups as well.

Today, it was tree planting. Suspicious fires last

season had left the hillsides burnt and bare, and the coven agreed that it was the right time for the new saplings to be planted.

"But why does it have to be me?" she grumbled, under her breath. "I've got books to shelve. Fingerprints to clean off windows."

"Where's your sister?" Dave McMillan, a school teacher and the head of the Ledstow Improvements Society, asked her. He leaned over to where a variety of digging implements were stuck into the soft grass.

Cara found a spade thrust into her grip. "I'm not sure. She said she was going to turn up."

"She went right past earlier. Well, it looked like her, at least."

Cara made a face. Up here? Serena would be safely down in town, somewhere, surely. But she had a twinge of uncertainty, not quite fear, at the top of her spine.

After working for about an hour, digging into the soft earth, gently wriggling the saplings out of their plastic bags and nestling them into their holes, Cara sat down for a rest at the edge of the plantation. A felled branch made a practicable seat and she lay her coat over it. Her stomach gnawed at her.

She pulled out her phone to ring her sister. Perhaps she could pick up some lunch for them on the way back.

The phone went straight to voicemail.

She stood up to try ringing again and noticed a flash of white. It appeared to be a snowdrop, fragile and elegant. Past that was a clump of daisies, then bluebells, and then an old-fashioned hellebore, or winter rose. She followed the curious trail of flowers, glancing behind again as the hush and fresh scent of the trees enveloped her. Had someone scattered a wildflower seed packet through here? She wasn't complaining. The flowers were a welcome distraction.

At the end of the trail were bright red Scarlet Elf Cup fungi, looking for all the world like they were holding their vessels up to be filled, and a line of toadstools beneath a tree covered in moss. She bent down to look, making sure not to get too close. Vague cautionary tales ran through her mind of fairy rings and kidnapping.

"I'm not that naive," Cara said, in a low voice, to no one in particular. "There's no way you'll catch me stepping into—"

The world fell away from beneath her feet in a sickening lurch. Falling, dropping, lost.

She flailed for an instant, in the between, as something resisted. Then she came through and her hand went up to her face as she landed at the edge of a lake so shiny it hurt to look at.

"— a fairy ring." Her voice came out in a whisper. "Oh, goddess."

In the other direction, she squinted to see that the plantation was gone and the forest around her was old and overgrown with moss and lichens. Huge tree trunks stretched to the sky and vines swung between them. Wild flowers crept between the trees; bluebells, daisies, and some large blooms she couldn't name. She smelt a musty scent, like the pot pourri in her grandmother's dresser.

The light had a sort of purple quality as if she was looking through tinted sunglasses. A waterfall streamed into the lake opposite her. Where was she? If she knew one thing, it was that this was not Ledstow. Not even England. The autumn damp feeling in the air was gone. She jumped up and looked carefully around.

A faint silver shimmer, like very fine glitter, hung over the ground where she had landed. A fairy tale. She was in a cursed fairy tale.

She walked back and forth over the spot, looking for the portal that she'd come through, then leaned back against a wide trunk. Her phone was nowhere to be found. Alright, this was fine. Fine.

An unfamiliar bird called a three-note call. Shadows were starting to creep through the clearing, and she shivered. Sitting at the edge of what looked like a large, forbidding forest was a silly thing to do. How many times had she railed at the main character in fantasy books for making stupid choices? She just needed to make a plan.

Water. She headed back towards the lake, bent down and scooped some cold water into her hands. Was it her imagination or was that the best, freshest water she'd ever tried? Perhaps a hint of melon…

"What are you?" A woman called from behind her. "And what are you doing in the Auld Forest?" The voice was friendly enough.

Cara turned. The Auld Forest. That answered the question of where she was, although it didn't help her much. The dark hood of her coat covered half of the woman's face and she had two small children, who were huddled behind her, clutching at her skirts.

"I'm a librarian," she said, rubbing at the spot on her hip where she had landed. "I didn't mean to end up here."

"Folk often don't," the woman said, and turned away.

"Wait. Please. I don't know how to get back."

"You can't. That way was just closing when you fell through."

"Yeah," one of the kids said, obviously feeling a little braver, as she came out from behind her mother. Fair hair framed a round face with pointed ears and large, round eyes. "Everyone knows that."

Cara approached the family. "Thank you," she said,

to the child, with a kind smile. "That's what I was worried about. Do you, perhaps, have a map?"

The child shook her head.

"No, we don't, but there are only two directions," the woman said, still speaking loudly as if Cara was hard of hearing. "Outward and — she pointed through the forest to where a huge, spreading tree towered above them all — magenward."

"I see," said Cara, although she didn't.

"Fancy being out in the forest during the float," the woman said to her kids, already turning away.

"Can she come with us, mama? She's got funny ears."

The woman turned around again, one hand on her hip. This was probably her best chance to find shelter. Cara put on her best 'welcome to the library' face that usually worked with anyone from kids to first timers.

"I'd be so grateful."

The woman paused. "I doubt you'd survive, otherwise."

READ MORE AT HTTPS://BOOKS2READ.COM/ATWIST

ABOUT THE AUTHOR

Kim Jackways is a freelance writer and mother based in New Zealand. She loves shady green places and teaching animals to talk. Her stories detail imaginary worlds filled with magic, with main characters who are somehow smarter and funnier than her.

Find K M Jackways online at www.kimjackways.com

ALSO BY K M JACKWAYS

REDFERNE WITCHES SERIES

Brand of Magic

Boundless Magic

Murmurs of Magic

Breaking into Magic

MUSICAL MAYHEM SERIES

Murder for a Song

Death and a Duet

Treble Death

TALES OF THE MAGEN SERIES

A Twist of Faerie